CLASH

COLIN MULHERN
CLASH

Catnip

CATNIP BOOKS
Published by Catnip Publishing Ltd
14 Greville Street
London EC1N 8SB

This edition first published 2011
1 3 5 7 9 10 8 6 4 2

A CIP catalogue record for this book is available from the British Library.

ISBN 978-1-84647-116-2

Printed in Poland

www.catnippublishing.co.uk

For Matthew
Jack
& Cameron

KYLE

I first saw Alex Crow in the toilets on my third day in secondary school.

At the time I had no idea who he was. He was just there, standing at the urinals while I was at the sinks with Gareth.

'I still hate coming in here,' said Gareth. He was picking his nose and trying to examine his nostrils, which wasn't easy considering the state of the mirror. It looked like every kid who ever came in here must have checked his reflection, gobbed on the glass and let it dry.

'They're just stories,' I said. 'Nothing's going to happen.'

But at that very moment the door slammed open and two older boys, big, strapping rugby types, burst in with a scream of, 'Newbies!'

They grabbed hold of Gareth, pulled him from the sinks, and had him flat on his back on the cracked floor tiles. His shirt came free of his trousers revealing a huge area of white gut.

'Ugh, look at him,' said one of the boys. He gave Gareth a kick. 'You fat slug.'

'Get up,' said the other thug. 'It's time for a wash, newbie.'

The two of them hauled Gareth back onto his feet.

I stood there in shock and terror, wondering at what point they were going to turn on me.

'Let's see if we can get some of that colour out of your hair, eh?'

Gareth had short, ginger hair. Not red or copper, or that pale, strawberry blonde that some people call ginger. Gareth's hair was orange. If you drew him, he'd look like a cartoon.

The first thug kicked open a cubicle, but Gareth managed to throw him off and grab the sides of the door.

'Move your arms,' shouted the other, punching him near the elbow. 'Move them!'

His mate was already back on Gareth and together they forced him into the open cubicle.

It was all frighteningly clear. Gareth was going to get his head flushed.

That was when the boy at the urinals, the other first year, zipped up his fly and turned to face us.

In an even, non-threatening tone, he simply said, 'Leave him alone.'

One of the thugs spat on the floor and said, 'Get lost, dickhead, or you'll be next.'

But the boy didn't move. He just stood there, as small and as thin as I was, with his hands in his pockets, watching.

All I could think was that he was mad. He certainly didn't look much compared to those other two but then I noticed the single gold stud earring in his left ear, a fat rusty-brown scab running along the right side of his forehead and the hint of an old scar on his chin.

But there was something else. His eyes. They were unusually wide – enough to make his pale grey irises float on their whites as he stared, unflinching, at the two older boys.

This was Alex Crow.

He didn't argue or threaten, and he didn't try to put on any kind of show at being hard or tough; he simply walked over and forced his way into the cubicle.

The first thug immediately released his grip on Gareth, pushing him clear. 'You little prick,' he said, as he reached out to grab Alex by the shirt.

Alex didn't try to stop him. He actually allowed the other boy to grab him, to pull him close. Not even a hint of a struggle. I'd never seen anything like it, but then I'd never seen anyone like Alex Crow, and at that moment I had no idea just how violent an eleven-year-old boy could be.

Without warning, Alex slammed his forehead into the centre of the older boy's face. Not just once, but again, and again, each blow vicious and accurate. As the first thug cried out and put his hands to his face, Alex turned on the other.

He didn't just punch with his fist; he used the heel of his hand, the back of his knuckles, as well as his knees and feet in a fast, effective and relentless attack. He even used the other boys' weight against them, putting one off balance, twisting out of the way and hauling him head first into the rim of the toilet bowl with a loud crack, then Alex was holding him by the back of his shirt, slamming his face down again while twisting to elbow the other boy in the throat.

When Alex finally stepped out from the cubicle he walked directly to the sinks, checked himself in the mirror and casually, carefully, washed his hands.

Gareth was staring at the boys in the cubicle. They were getting to their feet, their eyes switching from Alex to the exit, but they didn't make any move to leave.

As Alex dried his hands, I whispered to Gareth, 'Let's go.' But Gareth paused, tried to tuck his shirt into his trousers, then looked at Alex Crow.

'Thanks, man,' he said.

Alex stopped, as though he hadn't even noticed we'd been standing there. He sized up Gareth in a second. 'Say one word about this, you'll get a lot worse. Understand?'

Gareth's mouth dropped and he quickly nodded.

As I looked at Alex, I noticed again those eyes – wide and wild and grey – and I truly believed this boy had lost the plot.

•

The incident stuck with me, and for a long time I couldn't settle when I was out in the schoolyard – not until I knew that Alex Crow was nowhere near. Gareth was the same.

Usually Alex wasn't hard to find. He had a regular spot where he'd sit alone, staring into space with his back against the wall, one leg pulled up close, the other stretched out in front. He never gave us a second glance.

Then one day, Gareth suddenly nudged my arm. Alex was standing, about halfway between us and the tech block. He was looking right at me.

As Alex continued to stare, Gareth whispered, 'What do you think? Should we leg it?'

I couldn't answer. I could barely breathe through fear as I waited for Alex to come over and make his move.

But he didn't. He stayed just where he was. He watched me for another few seconds, then he lowered his eyes and rubbed the fingers of one hand with the other, as though considering something. Then he walked away.

'Jesus,' said Gareth. 'What the hell was all that about?'

Slowly, I shook my head. 'I've no idea.'

For the rest of that week, I was out of my mind with worry. I was convinced that some kind of attack was inevitable. I dreaded break times, but even more, I dreaded going home. The walk to the bus stop wasn't a long one, but it took all my self control not to continually look over my shoulder, wondering when Alex Crow was going to come running.

But he never did, which made me all the more uneasy about what had been going through his mind and why he had been staring at me for so long.

ALEX

I'll never forget the first time I saw Kyle. Some things just stick in your head.

There was a drawing on the wall of our art class. There were lots, obviously, but this one really stood out because it was clearly in the wrong area.

The art teacher had told us in our very first lesson, 'I hate the beginning of a new school year. Blank walls. So let's sort out this problem. Each year group will have a different area.' He picked up a metre stick and whacked the back wall. 'And this is yours, from here to the far end. We'll fill it up with classwork eventually, but for now, if you've got something at home, or fancy doing something before next week, bring it in, we'll take a look.'

There were six other classes in our year group, and only two art rooms. Over the next few days, pictures began to appear on the walls of both rooms.

And then the one that really stood out appeared. Not bang in the middle or anything obvious, just pinned up near the bottom, and when I saw it, it knocked me sideways. A copy of some album cover – pastels worked over in pencil – but it was in a league of its own, and it wasn't only me who thought so. One kid asked the teacher if it was a wind up.

It wasn't. He even gave us a name. That was enough for the others, but not me. I needed to find out who this kid was.

A few days later, someone pointed him out in the yard, so I wandered over to get a better look.

He was standing near the prefabs with some fat, ginger kid. I didn't know Gareth at the time, but recognised him from some incident in the bogs. I put that aside though. It was his mate I was interested in. I just kept thinking, that's him, that's the kid who drew that amazing picture.

Then he looked over. He seemed a bit edgy, like he expected me to go over and belt him.

I didn't, but I didn't look away either. I sort of felt that this kid was something special, you know? Something better than the rest. He had a genuine talent.

Like me.

Anyway, it was the next day that I nicked the picture. I wasn't a thief, not really, but I knew that someone was bound to steal it, and if that happened I'd never see it again. So I walked in, took it down, rolled it up and left.

KYLE

It didn't take long before Alex Crow's name started coming up again and again in conversation. I never said anything about what happened in the toilets, and I'm sure Gareth didn't either, but there was a lot of talk about a small, skinny boy in our year, who was a complete psycho. For some kids that was a challenge.

Kids like Matlock and Hughes.

Sean Matlock was tall and thin, Darren Hughes was a little shorter but stocky. They quickly established themselves as our class idiots; both as crazy as each other, and just as stupid. Best friends, but they fought constantly. They were the first in our class to get dragged out of assembly, the first to get detention, and when they heard about Alex Crow, they wanted to be the first to knock him down.

'I don't see what all the fuss is about,' said Sean. 'He looks a total weed.'

We were in the art room, probably the only lesson where I sat anywhere near these two. Sean was carving his name into the desk and Darren was flicking the dirty paint water at the window.

But Jamie Spencer had come from the same primary school as Alex, and he gave us the inside view. 'People avoided him in our school. He might not look much, but they were still pretty scared of him.'

Sean sneered, while Darren Hughes latched straight onto such ripe information. 'You saw him fight, did you?'

Jamie nodded. 'Now and again. He got excluded for it.'

'For fighting?' Darren shook his head. 'We had fights all the time in our school.'

'So did we . . . well not me. But this was different. A few weeks before we broke up, some kids were playing football on the field. Alex walked right into the middle, waited for them to react, and went wild.'

'He looks like a fairy to me,' said Sean.

Jamie's eyes returned to his work. 'He's an animal.'

Sean sniggered, spraying spittle over the desk. 'Yeah, right.'

'I'm telling you – he doesn't fight like other kids.'

Sean held up a fist. 'One solid smack from this . . .' He hit the table loud and hard. '. . . and he'll go down like a sack of shite. Trust me.'

•

Matlock and Hughes used to hang by the tech block with a bunch of other kids, mostly from the years above. They would slouch against the wall, spitting through their front teeth, swearing a lot, slagging each other off, occasionally sharing a hidden cigarette.

I'd expected Alex Crow to join this group too. From what I'd seen in the toilets that time, I thought he'd have been right at home. But he didn't. Alex kept to his same spot on the other side of the yard, sitting alone, gazing across the playground at nothing.

On several occasions, I noticed Matlock and Hughes staring over at him, sizing him up, then nodding and sniggering to their new friends. I once saw Alex look at them and noticed how they straightened up, ready for action. But Alex stayed where he was. Nothing happened.

Then one day, I spotted Alex coming out through the tech-block doors. This was about halfway through break time, so I guess he must have stayed back to finish off something. As he walked across the yard, Gareth mumbled next to me, 'I wonder what happened to him.'

Alex wasn't playing on it, but he definitely had a slight limp.

'I don't want to know,' I replied.

'It looks like he's got a black eye too,' said Gareth.

It wasn't a shiner, but it was definitely bruised.

Jamie Spencer was standing with us and put in, 'I'd hate to see the other kid.'

As he passed in front of the mob by the tech-block wall, I got a sudden sick feeling. I knew things were about to kick off. One of the older boys was saying something to Darren Hughes, egging him on. Darren pushed the other boy back and told him to get lost but Sean kept his eyes firmly on Alex. He was chewing on a matchstick, smiling to himself and nodding.

Without encouragement, he called out, 'Hey!'

Alex ignored him. He kept walking.

Sean grinned at his mates then stepped forward and called out a little louder, 'Hey, I'm talking to you.'

Alex stopped, turned and looked back.

Gareth grabbed my arm. 'Oh, man, there's going to be a fight.'

Sean took a step forward, head and shoulders above Alex Crow. He spat out his matchstick. 'What are you looking at, faggot?' He held his arms open, inviting a fight. 'You want your go? Come on then.'

Alex simply turned away and continued across the yard.

It was only then that I realised just how fast my pulse was going. And next to me, Jamie released the breath he must have been holding for nearly a minute.

'Jeezus,' he said. 'That was close.'

To Sean Matlock, it was a victory. He called out after Alex, 'Short-arsed little prick,' then turned back to his mates, gave the air a small punch and slapped Darren – matcho style – twice on the cheek. Darren slapped him back and within seconds they were knocking seven bells out of each other.

Over on the other side of the yard, Alex sat in his same old spot, alone, quietly watching Matlock and Hughes.

Sean Matlock was off school the following day and when he did return, despite a torrent of questions from Darren, he refused to talk about the bruise on the side of his jaw or the sling supporting his broken wrist.

ALEX

I think everyone's got a hidden talent – something they really shine at. I discovered mine when I was ten years old. I was in my last year of primary school; it was bank holiday weekend at the end of May. I know that, because I was at a barbecue at my uncle Joe's house.

Joe was a club owner. Two nightclubs, a snooker hall and a boxing club. He was my mam's big brother, and he really was big. Not just tall, but heavy and chunky. He drove a Jag – always gleaming – wore sovereign rings on his knuckles and a thick-link gold chain around his neck. His cheeks were always red and he spoke in this big, loud voice. He was pretty damn scary, but he was fun.

His house was on the outskirts of Durham, about a twenty minute drive from us. It was like a mansion, bloody enormous, spotlessly clean inside and out, with enough land that you could wander for hours without seeing another soul.

He had guns. Air rifles. He used to take us down to the bottom field where we'd shoot tin cans, old boots, or anything else we could use as targets.

Uncle Joe had a son called Neil – my cousin. He was four years older than me, tall and gangly with cropped hair. He was a right ugly sod. His spots would ooze puss and he wouldn't care. He always called me 'midget', and whenever he thought Joe was looking the other way, he'd belt me, slap me or beat me up. Sometimes he'd get away with it, other times he'd be seen. If it was my dad that caught him, he'd call over to me and say, 'Ah, just hit him back, you little girl,' but if it was Uncle Joe, he'd come over and give Neil a right mouthful – telling him not to pick on people half his size.

But on that day in May, things followed a different path.

It was a hot day – red hot – and we were all sitting out on the patio at the back of the house. My dad, small and wiry with his shirt off, was propped up against the stone wall next to the steps. He had a bottle of beer in his hand and was looking out at the open fields, occasionally waving away a fly with his free hand. My mam and Aunty Pat were sitting on sun loungers, covered in bronzing oil, gossiping and making their way through their first bottle of white wine. Me, I was sitting at the patio table, picking the ice cubes out of my lemonade and melting them in my hands, squeezing them till my fingers went numb.

So anyway, Neil came over and slumped into one of the chairs right next to me. I was expecting a typical Neil comment or a knock on the head as he leaned back in his chair, but for once he didn't even try. He never called me 'midget' either; he didn't kick me under the table; he didn't even pick his nose and flick snots at me. He just grinned and turned away, as if trying to hide a joke. I wanted to say something, but at that point Uncle Joe came out of the house carrying two air rifles and a box of pellets.

'Neil,' he shouted. 'Go and grab some cans.'

Aunty Pat looked up. 'Aren't you going to light the barbecue?' And she said it proper, like that – pronouncing 'going' like it was 'go-wing'. Having a big house made her try to sound posh. At least that's what my dad said.

Joe never tried to sound anything other than the way he was. He just smiled. 'Plenty of time for that, love. Thought we'd take the lads down the bottom field, shoot some targets.'

'Oh, brilliant,' I called. I was straight to my feet. Uncle Joe had let me shoot the air rifle earlier that year – just once – and I was dead keen to have another go. But as I stood up, I noticed Neil trying to conceal another grin.

My mam called out, 'Just be careful, will you?'

'We're always careful,' said Joe, and he put the guns in a large canvas bag, zipped it up and hitched it over his shoulder. He looked at my dad. 'You ready?'

My dad took a swig from his bottle. 'Yeah. Let's go.'

Neil had a bag of cans, just like Joe had asked for, and we all walked down towards the bottom field.

There was a line of trees down there, either side of a small brook, which separates that field from the top one. It's also a fair hike from the house, so with that, the trees and the curve of the land, once we were down there we were well out of sight of my mam and Aunty Pat.

Being so close to the brook, the midges were a real pain – clouds of the things, everywhere you turned – getting on your face and your mouth.

Neil ignored them and set up the cans on an old rusted oil drum. My dad was standing next to Uncle Joe, who had dropped the canvas bag but hadn't bothered to open it.

'Alex.' Joe spoke casually, scratching his hairy belly. 'Why don't you go and help your cousin set up those targets?'

'Will I get a go of the gun?' I asked.

'We'll see. Go on, you go and help Neil.'

And so I walked over, picked a can out of the bag and went to place it.

With a swing of his hand, Neil knocked the can flying.

'What do you think you're doing?' he snarled. And he stepped right up to me, gave me a shove.

I was taken by surprise and automatically pushed him away. 'Get off.'

'Make me.' And with both hands, he gave me a hefty push. I was knocked back, but I was still on my feet. I looked round to where my dad and Uncle Joe were standing. Surely they'd say something.

But they didn't. They just stood there, watching.

'Come on, midget.' Neil pushed me again. 'Make me.'

'Get off,' I said, and I pushed him back. I heard a slight laugh from behind — my uncle Joe — but before I got time to wonder what all this was about, Neil punched me.

It was the shock that really knocked me; the punch was fairly weak for Neil. It was the fact that he'd done it while Joe was standing there watching.

I expected Uncle Joe to blow his top, but it was my dad who spoke up, his voice ringing with annoyance. 'Well hit him back then.'

Joe chuckled and patted my dad on the shoulder. 'Give him a chance, Will.'

I looked up at Neil, hardly able to believe they were going to let him beat me up and watch him do it.

'Come on, midget,' said Neil. 'You just going to stand there, or what?' He lifted his fist to show he was ready to strike me again. There was only one thing I could do.

Hit the bastard.

So I did. I leapt forward and slugged him right across the jaw.

A second later I was on my back. My right eye was stinging like crazy and Neil was standing over me. Uncle Joe was roaring with laughter and my dad was shouting, 'Get up, lad.'

What the hell was going on?

'Help him up, Neil,' said Joe. And the next thing I knew, Neil was pulling me to my feet and asking if I was all right.

'You fight at school?' asked Joe, walking over towards me.

'Sometimes,' I said.

'You win?'

'Now and again.' I really wanted to add that putting me up against Neil wasn't exactly a fair fight.

Joe nodded and smiled. 'Well, it was a good punch, but if you've got someone like Neil here, it won't do you a lot of good.' He pulled Neil towards me. 'He'll win. Every time. Unless you know what you're doing, that is. So you tell me, Alex, what is the main difference between you and Neil?'

I shrugged. 'He's older.'

'Forget that. Age doesn't mean a thing. What else?'

'He's bigger.'

'Bingo. Or to look at it another way, you are smaller. And that's not a bad thing, Alex. You can use it to your advantage. Come here. Face Neil.'

My eye was still hurting, but I was intrigued by what was happening, so I did as I was told, wondering if it was something to do with Joe's boxing club.

'Now, Neil, stretch out your hand, like you were punching Alex here. Hold your hand still.'

Neil stretched out his fist towards me and held it there.

'See?' said Joe. 'See how he has to stretch down? That's because you're small. Now bend down a bit. There, see? If you get a little lower, you make it even harder for him to hit you. If you keep low, you keep safe. But in the same way, if you keep low, you can't hit him, can you? You need to get him down on the ground so you can get him on *your* terms. So how are you going to do that?'

I shrugged. 'Grab his legs?'

Joe smiled, clapped his hands and looked at my dad. 'See? What did I tell you?' Then he looked at me. 'Good lad, Alex. If you can pull his feet or his knees together, he'll go down. So go on, then. Go for it. Avoid Neil's punches and bring him down.'

Neil came to life, moving and punching the air, not to attack, but to make it more difficult for me. I kept what Joe had said in mind – keep low; avoid his fists; go for his legs.

Then I ran at him. I dived low and I wrapped my arms tight around his ankles. My knees were on the ground and I pulled at his legs with everything I had, ready to feel a crack on the back of my head any second.

But it worked. Neil fell over, and as soon as he hit the deck

I scrabbled round, got to my feet and did what I'd dreamt of for years. I gave him a kick, with everything I had, right in the ribs.

Of course, no sooner had I done that than he twisted round and grabbed me. He dragged me down on top of him and we rolled about, twisting, punching and kicking each other. It was real too, as real a fight as I'd ever had with Neil, but this time I didn't feel so picked on, and I didn't give up. I went for it, fighting back, feeling like I had half a chance of hurting the lanky git.

Above us, Uncle Joe was shouting encouragement and clapping his hands.

Neil eventually won the battle. He had my arm twisted behind my back and my face pushed against the ground. I couldn't move, but I was determined not to shout or scream.

Neil kept shouting in my ear, 'Submit. Submit.'

My dad yelled down at me, 'Do what he says, will you?'

Joe made it clear. 'Hit the ground three times, Alex. That's the sign.'

I did like he said – slap, slap, slap.

Neil immediately let go and helped me to my feet. His nose was bleeding – just a bit – but he was grinning. For the first time since I'd known my cousin, he was looking at me as though he actually liked me. He even shook my hand and said, 'You did good there, Alex. That was spot on.'

But what really made me feel proud was that when he said it, he didn't call me 'midget'.

He called me Alex.

•

I don't know how much my mam knew about this incident. Joe told us to wash off any blood in the little brook, and we managed to get some time for the guns, but we still must have looked a bit battered when we got back to the house.

If it did show, nothing was said, not by my mam, and not by Aunty Pat. They were well into their second bottle of wine and lost in conversation. The salad and snacks were all ready, and next to the barbecue was a huge tray of raw meat. All they were waiting for was for Uncle Joe to stick on his apron, put on his hat (with 'CHEF' printed on the front) and take control of the cooking.

The sun beat down, we stuffed our faces and the adults got drunk. When Neil passed me some cider, I did my best not to appear impressed, just saying, 'Cheers,' and taking a swig like it was nothing new.

But when he looked away I watched him. I took a good, long look at my cousin. Tall, ugly and about as evil as anyone I'd ever met. I found myself wondering if he'd *let* me bring him down, like it was all part of some game. But no. Neil was too arrogant for that. He'd never make anything easy for me. So no, there was no doubt about it. I'd done this myself. Me.

I might have been small and thin, but on that afternoon, with the sun and the cider and the smell of barbecue and sizzling meat, I felt like a giant.

After we'd eaten, Joe came over and asked how I was doing. I'd sneaked a few more swigs of cider and was feeling a touch dizzy, but I didn't admit to it. 'Fine,' I said.

He nodded, looked over at my mam and Aunty Pat, then said, 'You did well down in that field, Alex. Showed some real potential. Isn't that right, Neil?'

Neil nodded, his face straight. 'He did pretty good.'

Joe nodded. 'Surprised us all, I'd say.'

I wasn't sure whether to say thanks or not. Before I got the chance, he popped the question: 'How would you feel about some "proper" training?' He said it while picking bits of steak out of his teeth, not really looking at me, as though this was just general chat.

I sat up. 'Yeah. It'd be great.'

'You know where the boxing club is?'

'I think so.'

'You come there on a Tuesday night, seven o'clock, and you'll learn what real fighting is all about. You up for it?'

I was made up. This was brilliant. I guess I really impressed him down by the brook. 'You think I could be a boxer?'

Uncle Joe moved his head from side to side, weighing up an answer. 'Well, possibly, but for your size and weight I was thinking of something else.' And, still picking his teeth, he walked away.

I sat there, puzzled at what he meant, but Neil, who was still sitting next to me, leaned over and with a straight, mean face, he said, 'Ultimate Fighting. Like what I do.'

'What's Ultimate . . . ?'

His eyes narrowed. 'Anything you want. No holds barred. Kick, punch, wrestle. Better than boxing, any day. The *ultimate* sport.'

It sounded terrifying. 'You think I could?'

'No. But my dad does, and it's his club.'

•

Our trainer was called Carlos. He was short but broad with a fat neck and a bald head. Tiny blue tears were tattooed in the outer corners of his eyes and he was an expert in what he called 'Brazilian Street Fighting'.

He worked us hard. Pushing us until we couldn't take any more – press-ups on our knuckles, sit-ups, stretches. We thought our muscles would split and tear. Hurt like hell.

Carlos hammered home his rules, smacking one hand into the other. 'You keep these techniques *secret*. Got that? This style of combat does not have the hallmarks of a martial art. It looks messy. It looks undisciplined. Your opponent will think you're amateur, or scared, or clueless. All to your advantage. As far as your friends are concerned, you're doing kick-boxing or karate or bloody ballet dancing, I really don't care so long as you don't tell them what you're really doing here. And don't go showing off at school.'

We trained in a room upstairs, right above the boxing club. We could hear them below us, shouting and cheering each other on as they trained. I doubt they ever heard us though. The floor was covered in thick crash mats, and there were only ever a few of us there.

We all had regular partners. Neil trained with an older lad called Daniel. I trained with Carlos's son, who was about my age. At first, I thought he was brilliant. Fast. Agile. But after just a few weeks, I was faster. Even Carlos said so.

Most of the techniques were grappling – trying to get each other on the ground – and learning various holds and locks to make your opponent submit.

Carlos would pat us on the back for good work and crack us on the head for mistakes, and he would end every session with his golden rule of secrecy.

The thing is, it's hard to keep to a rule like that, because back at school the gymnasts were forever practising cartwheels and handstands, the footballers were dribbling and shooting, there was even a kid who could juggle and every day he'd be chucking three balls in the air. And so it was only natural that I began to test my own skills. At the club I was constantly being told how good I was, how I had natural talent. I wanted to know if they were right.

And so, with only four or five weeks training behind me, I tried it out. I went looking for an argument and had the other kid on the deck before he knew what was happening.

I thought maybe it was luck, so I upped the stakes and tried someone else.

He screamed so loud that I ended up losing my break time for the following two days. Didn't matter. While the teacher threw words at me, bawling out her disgust – even though the other boy was bigger than me – I just stood there and stared right back. I didn't smile, I didn't blink. I'd won. And that's all that mattered.

I was a small, skinny kid – proper little short arse, but during that last term in primary school, I started to build quite a reputation. And, yeah, the teachers began to notice, but so what? It felt good.

I decided to mark my eleventh birthday with something special.

At dinner time, I strolled onto the field, right in the middle of a football game. First came the shouts to move, then the names, then the full-on challenges.

Bring it on.

By the time the teachers got to me, I'd caused enough carnage to get myself in a whole heap of trouble.

Not only did I get excluded, but we had the headmaster, social workers and god-knows-what coming round our house to 'discuss' things.

When they turned up, my mam had to hide her booze, do as she was told and keep her mouth shut. While they sat on the sofa with folders and sheets of paper, my dad sat right on the edge of his chair. Every now and again he'd look in my direction, and he was constantly twitching, clearing his throat, scratching the backs of his hands as the other adults talked. As far as he was concerned the whole lot of them were only one step from the police.

He played the part of the concerned parent pretty well though and he made me promise, right there in front of them all, that nothing like this would happen again, that from now on it was work, work, work. He'd make sure I'd keep my head down, my nose clean. He said that education was too important to squander, and he even thanked them for coming and shook their hands as they left.

It was two weeks later, once I was back at school and he was sure there weren't going to be any surprise visits, that my dad made his move.

He was sitting in his armchair, waiting for me.

'How was your day at school?' he said, getting to his feet.

'All right,' I muttered.

I'd hardly got the words out when he grabbed me by the arm and dragged me towards the kitchen.

'Go easy on him, Will,' my mam shouted.

He snapped at her to stay right where she was and pushed

me through the kitchen and out through the back door. He tried to give me a crack with the back of his knuckles. It was pure instinct for me to dodge and he missed by a mile.

He bared his teeth. 'Stand still, boy,' and I had to stand my ground while he whacked me across the side of my head. Then he pulled me close, pressed his face right against my ear so that his stubble was scratching my cheek and he said, 'If I ever, *ever* get those people round our house again, it won't just be a crack on the head you'll get. There's a time for fighting. A time and a place. Do you understand that, boy?'

I nodded, expecting another crack. 'Yeah.'

Because I did understand. Carlos had already told me.

He was talking about the cage. And by the time I was in secondary school, I knew all about it.

KYLE

The rest of my first year in secondary school was pretty much incident free as far as Alex Crow was concerned. We'd see him in the yard, of course, but he usually kept himself to himself. Matlock and Hughes didn't really bother with him either; there were too many other kids to fight with or pick on.

In the summer term our form teacher announced a trip to Northumberland. 'It's a four-night stay, and an opportunity to experience some outdoor activities we can't offer at school – rock climbing, canoeing, orienteering . . .' He handed a pile of pamphlets for us to share out. 'But there are limited places, so get your names in fast.'

Gareth wasn't too keen. 'Can you see me in a canoe?'

'What are you talking about? They'll just give you a bigger one. Adults canoe, don't they? Come on, it'll be a laugh.'

'I thought you didn't like outdoor sports.'

I waved the pamphlet at him. 'It's not sport, is it? Look. Hill walking, rock climbing, abseiling. It'll be great.'

Gareth looked at the pamphlet, but he didn't seem convinced.

'No school. No homework. Staying up late at night, midnight feasts, crisps, pop.'

Gareth merely raised an eyebrow. But I knew I was getting somewhere. Eventually he agreed and put his name down.

•

Alex didn't go on the trip, but Matlock and Hughes did. They were at the back of the coach and started with their jibes from the off.

'Hey, Kyle,' shouted Darren. 'Hope you don't have to hold Gareth's rope when he's rock climbing.'

'Funny,' said Gareth.

'Heeeave,' called Sean, through cupped hands.

I felt a surge of anger, turned and tried to put them both in their place. 'Yeah, well I hope you're not standing *under* him.'

And then I realised what I'd said.

Oh shit.

Matlock and Hughes howled with laughter, adding, 'Spur-latt!' and 'Anyone brought a footy pump to pump us back up?'

I whispered to Gareth, 'Sorry, man. I didn't mean it like that.'

'Yeah, cheers, *mate*. I can fight my own battles, you know.'

I felt terrible.

Matlock and Hughes kept sniggering and passing comments and sound effects, but after a while they moved onto someone else.

I tried to think of something to say to make up for it, went over thoughts and apologies, eventually turning to say a simple, 'Sorry.'

Gareth was just sitting there, looking down at the foot rest like he hadn't even heard me.

'Gareth? You OK?'

He snapped his head up. 'Hmm? Yeah.' Then he surprised me with a grin. 'I'm fine.'

He looked over at Sean Matlock, and then in a voice loud enough that only two or three other kids nearby could hear, he said, 'Some kid who came here last year, he saw the ghost. Scared him so much, he had to be taken home.'

There were a few reactions of, 'A ghost?' and 'What, where?' But it wasn't long before someone else said, 'I heard about that too. It was on the stairs.'

Then someone else added, 'It's an old man.'

'No,' said a girl even further away. 'It's a kid who died rock climbing. He forgot to tie his rope right.'

'It's a woman, a local witch. She comes in the night looking for someone to take back with her.'

And on and on.

Gareth leaned towards me and whispered, 'By the time we get there, they'll be well and truly primed.'

'Primed for what?'

Gareth didn't answer. He just sat back and looked out of the window.

•

The house had four main dormitories. Two upstairs for the girls. Two downstairs for the boys. It was a race for the top bunks, but two of the winners were ejected by Matlock and

Hughes. Sean Matlock ended up in the bunk directly above me. I was gutted, wondering at what point in the night he would lean over and belt me with something.

After lights out, I braced myself, but Sean was more involved in conversation about the next day and the things we'd be doing, boasting about how great he'd be, how easy everything was. This went on for fifteen minutes or so, but eventually there was a lull in the conversation.

Here it comes, I thought. *Any second now, a pillow is going to hit me right in the face.*

But instead, from the bunk on the opposite side of the dorm, Gareth's quiet voice cut through the darkness. 'This is just like that house those hikers found.'

A few replies of, 'What?', 'Which hikers?' and 'What did he say?', 'Yeah, speak up, Gareth.'

'It was in the paper,' said Gareth, speaking a little clearer, a little louder. 'About two months back. Two hikers got lost on the hills near here. It was getting dark and it was raining, like *really* raining. They had only come out for the day, so they had no tent or torch or anything. They thought if they ended up spending the night on the mountain, they would probably die of hypothermia.'

Someone uttered, 'Whoa.'

Another said, 'Can that happen?'

Gareth's voice came back, 'Oh yeah. They needed shelter, and fast. Anyway, they were in luck, right, because they saw a light in the distance. A single square of light – a window – which meant a house. As they got closer, they noticed that the light was flickering.'

'Flickering?'

34

'Yeah. It was flickering. They realised it must have been candlelight. Maybe the house didn't have electricity or something, because it was in the middle of nowhere. By this time, it was pitch black and they were drenched to the skin, so this house was their only hope. They went right up to the door, and as they knocked, it slowly swung open.'

We could hear muffled laughter and fighting from the other dormitory, but in ours, everyone was listening with bated breath.

Gareth continued. 'One of the hikers shouted up the stairs, "Hello? Anyone here?" but there was no reply.

'"They must be flat out asleep," said the other hiker. He felt for the light switch, but they were right – no electricity. So they were left thinking, should we leave, or should we go upstairs and see if we can wake someone up?'

'Shit,' said one kid. 'I definitely wouldn't go upstairs.'

'And neither did they,' said Gareth. 'Instead they decided to just kip down in the front room. At least they'd be out of the rain and could just explain in the morning.

'So they walked into the front room. It was pitch, pitch black in there, and just a few steps into the room, the first hiker tripped over something on the floor. He nearly smashed his face open on the fireplace. The other hiker said it was too dangerous to wander about, that they should just find a spot and lie down. And that's exactly what they did.'

Gareth paused. No one said a word.

'Next thing they knew, it was morning, and outside they could hear police sirens and cars screeching to a halt. Suddenly there were police everywhere, *armed* police. One had a gun pointed right at them, yelling, "Stay where you are. Don't move."

'That's when they saw the bodies.

'Two other hikers had rented that house. One was lying across the floor – he was what the first hiker had tripped over. The other was slumped on the sofa. Both had been decapitated. Their heads had been placed squarely on the mantelpiece, their eyes rolled up, mouths half open.'

'What?'

'No way!'

'There was blood everywhere, splattered up the walls, dripping down the fireplace, and above them, the hikers could hear shouts and a struggle in the bedroom upstairs. It took three officers to arrest him – a lunatic, escaped from a nearby asylum. And as they tried to drag him out of the house, he looked in the front room, clawing at the door, and screamed, "AREN'T YOU GLAD YOU DIDN'T WAKE ME UP!!!"'

When Gareth cried out those last words, everyone in our dormitory jumped.

Then came the laughter, the swearing.

It was dark in the dormitory, but I could make out Gareth, and could see him grinning like a Cheshire Cat.

And then the questions: 'Is that true?', 'Did that really happen?'

'No way,' said someone else. 'You made that up.'

Sean Matlock, just above me, quietly muttered, 'Yeah.'

'Was it really in the paper?'

Gareth didn't answer. He just lay there smiling. And I knew why. When Gareth said something like that, that it was on the news or in all the papers, I knew it was time for a scare story. He called them urban legends, and he had loads of them. So I egged him on. 'Tell us another one, Gareth.'

Gareth twisted on his bunk. 'You want another?'

'Yeah,' came one reply, followed by, 'Go on then.'

'No,' said Matlock. 'Let's just get to sleep, eh?'

But he was outvoted by the shouts for more.

'OK,' said Gareth. 'But this one's *really* scary . . .'

•

When we got back to school we got notice of our new classes for the following year. This was called banding, and depending upon your ability and achievements in the first year, you would be in top, middle or bottom band.

Matlock and Hughes were over the moon to find they were in the bottom band, claiming it was by far the best deal because the work was dead easy and you could just muck about.

Jamie Spencer was devastated to find he was in the middle band and started to insist that his father would be straight down to the school to correct this glaring error.

Gareth gave a whoop and slapped me on the arm. 'We're in top!' We couldn't help jumping about and cheering at our success; we were even in the same form.

Jamie took exception to this and decided he'd piss on our parade by pointing to a name we hadn't noticed and in an acid tone, he said, 'Yeah, but you get the school psycho in your class.'

As he said this, Alex Crow stepped up behind him.

Something in our expressions told Jamie to shut up. He turned to see what was wrong. When he realised Alex had heard every word, he looked like he was going to cry.

Alex simply winked. 'I made the top. That's all that matters.'

I slipped away and Gareth came with me.

Checking to make sure Alex wasn't following, I said, 'At least we've lost Matlock and Hughes.'

'Some swap,' replied Gareth. 'Matlock and Hughes are just clowns. Jamie was right – Alex Crow really is a psychopath.'

'Well he got in the top band. He can't be that bad.'

'Just means he's an intelligent psychopath. That's even worse.'

Over the next few weeks we went round in circles over how bad our class would or wouldn't be. But soon enough the summer break was upon us, and I had something that took my mind off Alex Crow completely.

ALEX

It was just a few weeks after my exclusion when I came face to face with the cage.

At the club, the cage was all they ever talked about.

'Being in that cage, man. Total adrenalin rush.'

'Best thing you ever experienced.'

'Just you and your opponent, locked inside.'

'Ultimate fighting!'

They laughed when I asked why I couldn't go and watch. Daniel patted me on the shoulder like I was some stupid child. 'Doesn't work like that, sunshine. It's not what you call a family event. It's not exactly a prime location either. It all goes on in an old warehouse. It's kind of hush-hush, you know, so invited guests only. And the only time you'll be invited is if you're fighting. If you're not going in the cage, then you're not invited.'

Neil laughed. 'What's the matter, Alex? You look worried.'

'No I don't.'

'Well you needn't be. Carlos knows what he's doing. He won't put you in there unless he thinks you'll win.'

Daniel added, 'And Carlos reckons you're nearly there.'

'Really?' This was doing wonders for my ego.

'Really. Not everyone is up to cage fighting, but Carlos reckons you could be some kind of friggin' prodigy.'

Whether they had been told to say all this, or they were doing it off their own backs, it did the trick because a few weeks later, when Carlos said, 'Alex. You're up next Friday. It's time to see what you're made of,' I was so excited I would have taken on the world.

•

The warehouse was down by the river.

In the car, my dad gave me a short lecture on the location, about it being part of the old shipyards and about how he got his first job down there.

'I was a labourer – carrying stuff, doing a bit of this, bit of that. Course that was before I got this trouble with my back – can't do fuck all these days . . .'

To be honest, I drifted off. I kept my face to the window, looking out into the night, watching the scenery change from houses and shops and streetlights to factories – closed for the night behind chain-link fences, the odd security guard walking a dog and smoking a cigarette. We kept going to the farthest end of the industrial estate where the factories were boarded up, tagged with graffiti. The car parks were strewn with litter, ridden with weeds and the only vehicles were the burnt-out shells of stolen cars. None of this did anything to ease my nerves. I tried to remind myself that I wouldn't be here if Carlos didn't think I was ready. It wasn't much comfort.

We came off the road and parked in an area of flattened ground covered with rubble and broken glass. There were other cars there, but no signs on the actual warehouse to say we'd got the right place. The only indication that something was going on was the light above a small red door with a bouncer standing guard. He nodded to my dad as we walked towards him, opening the door to let us in.

The very first thing I saw was the cage.

It stood on a raised stage in the centre of the warehouse; an industrial altar of heavy-duty wire fencing. Eight walls, two metres high, bolted together to form an octagonal cage. The steel dead-bolt that locked the only door was monstrous, rusted and somehow buckled. Up above, raw cables were snaked and twisted around a horizontal beam, feeding the high-power spotlights that shone down, illuminating the cage, the battered mesh walls, and the streaked padding of a canvas floor.

I swallowed and looked around the rest of the warehouse. It was pretty basic. Cheap, plastic chairs and tables surrounded the stage. There were people sitting here and there; dark shapes smoking, drinking, talking and lit up by the occasional flash of a lighter. There was a makeshift bar at the back of the room with crates of beer stacked up behind it. Next to the bar, there was a small DJ stand. There were two changing rooms and a toilet on the opposite side of the room, and that was pretty much it. The whole place had a rancid, stale smell that made me feel sick to my gut and made my nerves all the worse.

Joe met us at the bar. He got my dad a drink, asked me if I wanted a coke and then what I thought about seeing the cage for the first time.

'It's scary,' I said.

Joe took a drink, his eyes never leaving me. 'It's a lot scarier on the inside.'

I tried not to swallow, disguising it by looking about the warehouse and quickly realised the cage wasn't the only thing that was scary in there – the punters for instance. They ranged from scarred and tattooed steroid monsters to wiry, sharp-tempered, fidgety characters like my dad. They all looked like gangsters or villains of one kind or another, and Uncle Joe seemed to know them all. As they came over to the bar they would either nod to him as they passed, or shake his hand and wish him well.

I expected the conversations to be about dirty deals or bank jobs, but instead they were open, friendly – just like any conversation you'd hear in any regular place. I remember one guy, taller than Joe and broad as a house. He had a brown leather jacket, a close-cropped beard and a voice like gravel. 'You got something special lined up tonight, Joe?'

'I always have something special lined up,' said Joe. He shook hands with this monster and added, 'How's your boy doing?'

'Got us up every night.'

'Well I hope you're doing your bit – changing nappies, bottle-feeding.'

'Hey, look at me. I'm a modern man. I even get his wind up and take him to the park.'

'Be a few years till you bring him here, eh?'

The other bloke managed a smile. 'Yeah, let's save that misery for a few more years, eh?'

Joe laughed. 'He'll be in the cage before you can blink.' Then he clapped his hand on my shoulder and said, 'Take my nephew here, young Alex. It's his first fight tonight. Seems like yesterday when I could hold him in one hand.'

The other guy looked down at me and raised an eyebrow. 'Looks like you still could. Bit small, isn't he?'

'Small and fast. Small and fast. I've got him up against some kid from the north side. Should be a good little match. Anyway, nice to see you. Go get yourself a beer. I'll catch you later.' Then he turned to me. 'You too, Alex, I've got things to do. Enjoy the night, and when you're in there, put up a good fight.'

As he walked away, the DJ knocked up the music and my dad pulled me towards the seats. 'Come on, lad. The show's about to begin.'

•

The entertainment began with the dancers.

Rock music blared out through speakers and two women, wearing nothing but sexy, frilly, frothy underwear, walked into the cage. One was in black, the other in red and they danced around the cage with twists and turns and high kicks. But what was really weird was as they danced – apart or together – the audience didn't cheer or applaud. They didn't shout or jeer or laugh or anything. I looked about to see some men just sitting there, watching, drinking. Others were taking no notice, chatting, exchanging money.

I looked back at the dancers to see them taking each other's tops off.

My dad gave me a nudge in the side. 'Close your mouth.'

I blinked, looked back at the stage, shut my mouth and swallowed. The show was certainly mesmerising, but equally uncomfortable – especially with my dad sitting right next to me. Deep down, I kept thinking, nearly over . . . nearly over.

A moment later my dad nudged me again. 'Stop staring and get yourself ready.'

There were no changing rooms for the junior fighters, only for the adults. I suppose we were seen as a cabaret act, something between the dancers and the main fighters – a way of warming up the audience – so we were expected to arrive at the warehouse ready to go. Either that, or we were to get changed where we sat.

I took off my jacket, pulled off my top and unzipped my jeans. I already had the shorts on. No need for boxing boots or anything flash; we fought barefoot.

When the dancers left the cage, the MC for the evening – an old, rough-looking guy called Jim Banks – picked up a microphone and announced the first fight.

'OK, lad,' said my dad. 'You ready?'

'Yeah. I think so.'

He pointed to some dumpy-looking kid who was standing at the side of the cage. 'You see him over there? That's your opponent. Chubby little fucker, eh? You'll nail him, boy, no sweat.' He smiled and gave me a wink.

This wasn't like my dad at all, and for some reason it jarred me. I took another look at that other kid, and I knew he wasn't anything special, but I got a serious touch of nerves. Everything seemed to bear down on me; the cage, the audience, the music, the dancers and that terrible stale smell.

It all seemed to be saying the same thing – I shouldn't be here. This was no place for someone my age. I might have been good at the club, with Carlos training me, or at school, but here, surrounded by nightmares . . . I was out of my league. The people sitting around the cage were expecting a proper fight, not two eleven-year-old kids just playing the part.

The MC had already announced the name of my opponent. A moment later I heard him say, 'And from Penshaw, another new fighter, Master Alex Crow.'

The audience clapped and cheered.

My dad gave me a shove. 'Go on then. Get in there.'

Again I hesitated and the MC repeated, 'Master Alex Crow. Is he here?'

My dad bit his lip, then leaned close and said, 'Go on, son. You'll murder him.'

And for some reason, that did the trick. I'd never had my dad treat me like this before. He'd never been proud of anything I'd done – I don't think I'd ever done anything he would be proud of, but all of a sudden I had this. All I had to do was go up there, leather that kid, and my dad would *really* be proud. He'd cheer and he'd clap, he'd slap me on the back and buy me chips on the way home and it would feel like he was a proper dad, maybe even a friend.

I walked into the cage.

•

It didn't start well. The audience gave me a hard time because I'd taken so long to get up there. A few laughed, taking the piss about my size, that I looked too young. The MC held his hand up to quieten them.

'Calm down, calm down. We've all got to start somewhere.' Then he turned to us. 'OK, boys, no biting, no gouging. Other than that, no holds barred. When the bell goes, start fighting.'

Then he ordered us to our corners and retreated from the cage. The door slammed shut and a bolt locked home.

The other kid hardly even glanced at me. He kept looking into the audience, perhaps trying to find his own dad. His eyes glanced up at the lights, to the cage door and then back to the audience. But not once did he look at me, not until the bell went.

I walked towards the centre, my hands guarding like Carlos had taught me. The other boy had a similar stance, but his arms were wobbling and he was white as a sheet.

A shout rang out from the audience – someone yelling the other boy's name. It was enough to distract him and I took a swing, and then another and another. This was nothing like fighting in the schoolyard – I felt a surge of panic and gripped onto the feeling of victory. I was laying punch after punch and so far, he hadn't hit back. It hardly registered that my hands were wet. I don't even think I noticed the smell – all I could think of was winning, getting out of the cage and having my dad cheer and punch the air and shout, 'Yesss!' So I kept swinging and punching and he was up against the wall of the cage and the audience were shouting . . .

And then hands were on my shoulders, pulling me away.

Jim Banks, the MC, was in the cage with us. Something was wrong and he was leading me away from the other boy. My hands and my chest were wet, and finally I realised what that smell was.

The other boy had been sick. Nerves had got to him too.

As soon as I had thrown that first punch, he'd vomited – over me, over himself. But worse than that, he'd kept vomiting, and I'd kept hitting him. I was so wrapped up in winning the fight that I'd never realised he was choking. They'd rung the bell twice – but I was so blinkered that I hadn't heard. I only realised something was wrong when there were other people in the cage, pulling me away.

•

He was all right. The other kid. He didn't die or anything. And as someone – either his dad or a coach – wiped him down with a towel and tried to tell him he'd done well, he looked more annoyed than ill. Someone else came in to check him over, then gave Jim a nod. The others left the cage and the MC brought us together. He lifted my arm in the air and announced me as the winner. There were a few boos and someone shouted, 'Disqualify him,' but the MC stood by his decision, told us to leave the cage and announced the next junior fight.

And that was it. That was my first match, and the first time it felt like my dad had really supported me. It was the first time I genuinely felt he believed in me, and now I'd done it, now I'd been in the cage, he would be really proud of me.

But when I left the cage, he wasn't there to greet me. He wasn't there to cheer and slap me on the back.

I eventually found him near the bar talking to some fat bloke.

'Dad?'

He glanced round. 'What?'

'I won.'

'Yeah, I know.' The other man handed my dad some money. My dad quickly counted it, nodded, then took more money from his wallet and handed it across. The fat man grunted then turned away to deal with someone else.

My dad stuffed the rest of the money in his wallet and looked round at me.

'What are you doing over here?' he said with a frown. 'Go and sit down before we lose our seats. Bloody hell, boy, I've got fifty quid on the next one.'

Because that's all he was interested in – the next bet.

He wasn't even interested in the fighting. I know, because as the weeks went on, I used to watch other punters and how they reacted to the fights. Uncle Joe was a good example. He'd sit back, smoking a cigar the size of a baby's arm, a drink in his hand and he'd be laughing and cheering. When a fighter made a good move, Joe would be on his feet, shouting, cheering, clapping his hands. When they did something he didn't like, he'd curse and yell insults.

But my dad . . . He would just sit there, chewing his nails, staring with wide eyes, occasionally spitting through gritted teeth. The only sign of enjoyment was when the fighter he'd backed got a good shot, and even then all he'd do was take a single drink from the bottle he was holding. The only time he got to his feet was when the MC announced the winner, and that was only to settle the score and place another bet.

So much for the proud dad.

He never bought me chips on the way home either. He should have done. Especially as time went on because I won almost every fight I was put up for, and I made him a lot of money. OK, I never made him rich, but I got used to him counting a wad of cash when I came out of the cage. The least he could have done was show his gratitude – I don't mean that I wanted him to buy me a bike or anything. I just wanted him to say thanks, or tell me how good I was – something to make me feel good, you know?

But it never happened. I suppose I should have been gutted, or thrown in the towel and told him to sod it, but with every fight I got a bigger buzz, and with every win I got a bigger cheer. The manic desire to win was taken over by confidence, by focus, accuracy. Technique kept that manic side under control. Carlos hammered me over this, insisting on control and strategy and never, ever to let anger take over.

He was right. And pretty soon the reputation I'd had at school was rekindled in the cage, and I couldn't care less whether my dad was proud or not.

The months rolled by and the fights went on. My opponents got bigger and faster, but I still won. In fact, as far as the fights were concerned, it was all going well – brilliant, in fact.

Right up to the night that Jim Banks was murdered.

KYLE

My mum had her share of boyfriends, but not so many that it felt odd. Most, I never got to meet and those I did, didn't spend much time with me.

Robbo, with his long hair, earrings and black leather waistcoat, was different. He'd ask me about school, TV and stuff. He'd even tell me jokes. But what really tipped the balance in Robbo's favour were his tattoos. He had them on both arms – snakes and thorns twisting and weaving from his wrists to his neck, multi-coloured stars scattered in the gaps, webs, skulls – all kinds of things. As I examined them, my mum mentioned that I was a bit of an artist myself.

'Really?' said Robbo, sounding genuinely impressed. 'I'd love to see some.'

I'd actually been dying for an excuse to mention my pictures, to bring something down to show him, but when he said that, I felt all stupid. I thought he'd see my pictures and just laugh.

I mumbled something about them not being all that good – not really. My mum cut in, 'Oh, that's nonsense, Kyle. You know you're good.' She turned to Robbo. 'He is.' Then she gave me a nudge. 'Go on, Kyle. Go and get some. You know you want to.'

I shuffled out of the room, but when I came back, I had my whole folder.

Robbo was knocked out. 'These are amazing!' He went through my work page by page, remarking on sketches and unfinished stuff like it was real art. 'I mean it,' he said. 'Totally amazing.' He clicked his fingers and pointed at me. 'Tell you what, when we make it big, we're going to need a cover for our CD. You fancy it?'

'What? Do the cover? Yeah. I mean, wow. Yeah.'

My mum was giggling behind her wine. 'Perhaps in a few years.'

'No,' said Robbo. 'He could probably do it now. Seriously. These are well mint. You fancy doing a backdrop? At the minute we've got a big sheet of cardboard with our name on. We need a proper logo. You up for it?'

'I don't think I've got any paper big enough.'

'Don't worry about that. It's the design that's important. You come up with that and I can get someone else to blow it up full size.'

I was beaming. I ran back upstairs, cleared my desk, and set to work.

About two hours later, my mum came to my room.

'You're not going to work on that all night, are you?'

'Well, no. Not *all* night.'

She came over, picked it up. 'It's very good.'

'I can't believe he asked me to do a CD cover. I mean, imagine what it'll be like when he makes it big, when everyone at school knows who he is.'

'*If* he makes it big.' With her free hand, she rubbed my hair – the way she did when she thought I was saying something stupid. 'Robbo is very nice, and he's very enthusiastic about the band. But I think it's going to be a while before he turns up in a limousine.'

I looked at my sketches and roughs, and I thought about the time I'd already spent. 'Do you think he was joking about the backdrop?

'I don't think he was joking. Not in a bad way. Maybe he was just trying to get in your good books, talk about art and stuff. Make friends.'

I frowned. 'He said the backdrop they have at the minute is rubbish.'

She handed back my picture. 'I wouldn't know.'

•

Two days later, Robbo was back. I didn't hear him come in but I heard my mum's voice, so I knew she must have been talking to someone.

It sounded like she was having a right go at him. By the time I got downstairs it had developed from a talk, to a heated debate, to a rant. I very nearly went back upstairs but Robbo noticed me standing in the hall, and he saw the sheet of paper in my hand.

'Hey, Kyle, man. That's not our backdrop, is it?'

My mum looked furious. 'Robbo. Don't.'

'I'm just having a look. Come here, mate. Give me a look.'

It wasn't quite the atmosphere I'd imagined. A little reluctantly, I handed over the design.

Robbo's face lit up. 'Whoa, Kyle. You did this?'

'Erm, well, yeah. You like it?'

'Like it? Man, this is great. Pure class-in-a-glass, Kyle. Seriously. This is exactly what we're after.' He showed my mum. 'What do you think? Think it'll look good?'

My mum shrugged. 'If you say so.'

'Oh, come on. It will. I'll get Nick to copy it full size. We'll have it ready for the gig on the 13th. And I don't care what you say. You're coming.'

My mum didn't look happy. Not one bit. '*She'll* be there, won't she?'

'Of course she will. She's our singer.' He put his hands on both my mum's shoulders. 'Look, nothing happened. You know that. Don't you?' My mum was looking down and Robbo had to bend down to catch her eyes, make her smile. 'You know that. See? So what do you say? You'll come, yeah?' He looked at me. 'Kyle too. He'll love it.'

'He's twelve years old.'

'It's cool. The pub landlord's an old mate. Besides,' he held up my design. 'Kyle's practically part of the band now.'

I couldn't believe what I was hearing. 'I can go and see you play?'

My mum snapped, 'No!'

'Maybe,' said Robbo. 'We'll talk it over.'

'He's not going.'

Robbo pulled my mum close. 'Come here,' and gave her a hug.

Over her shoulder, he gave me a wink.

I saw a lot more of Robbo over the next few weeks. He gave me a demo tape, mentioned the gig and the backdrop, 'Nick's on it now,' he said. 'Copying it with spray paint. Gonna look fantastic, man.'

He talked a lot about Nick. Nick was their bass player but he was their manager too. He had all kinds of plans for the band. Robbo would talk about these endlessly while my mum smiled and rolled her eyes. He mentioned the band's lead guitarist too, but never their singer. And the more he talked about the others, the more I got curious about this singer my mum had only referred to as '*she*'. So one day, when my mum was out of the way, I asked him.

'Lydia?' he replied. He checked the door and lowered his voice. 'Oh, you'll like Lydia. She's nasty.'

•

I'd only ever been to pubs that served meals. The sort of places with babies screaming in high chairs, toddlers fighting, mums and dads shouting at them or complaining about the prices.

The pub Robbo took us to couldn't have been more different. It was dark, dingy and smelly. The floor was sticky. The walls had posters pasted over other posters, guitars were sunk into the plaster on the walls, along with a thousand cracked CDs, picture frames (with no pictures) and the occasional stone gargoyle. Everyone in that place had either long hair, spiked hair, or no hair at all. It was a sea of leather and studs, and the music playing on the jukebox was loud, aggressive and riddled with bad language.

I thought my mum would go spare, but she just laughed, asked me if I was all right and if it was loud enough.

'Ta-dah.' Robbo appeared behind us. He handed a bottle of beer to my mum, a coke to me. 'What do you think, Kyle?'

He was pointing to the backdrop. *My* backdrop. It was right there behind the drumkit, for everyone in that pub to see – bold, silver letters at the top of a black sheet, with red claw marks tearing down below. Simple, but effective.

'The whole band love it,' he yelled. Then he leaned close and added, 'Especially Lydia.' He gave me a wink. 'Just try to keep your eyes inside your head, eh?'

The band were loud, fast and raw. In fact, they were so loud it was hard to make out much of anything. Robbo was an animal behind the drum kit, hitting those things like he was trying to destroy every one. The bass player was forever standing on the amps. The lead guitarist spent most of his time bent over in a knot, playing the hell out of his Flying V.

But my eyes were mainly on the singer.

Whatever she was wearing, it was shiny, black and very tight. Her arms and shoulders were bare. Her fishnet tights had holes ripped in them, and her boots were big, monster things with horns and silver clasps.

She kept flicking her long black hair over her shoulders, holding the microphone in one hand and looking sultry. Then she'd grab the mic stand with her free hand, lean right over the crowd and scream lyrics at them. She was terrifying, malevolent, *evil*, but absolutely beautiful.

They played four songs then left the stage, leaving the audience to cheer and scream for more.

Robbo came back first, thumping the bass drum. The entire pub clapped in time, keeping the beat going for what must have been an age. My palms were killing by the time the rest of the band returned.

And then they tore into something even louder and faster than before.

•

As we made our way to the taxi rank, my mum asked me what I thought.

'Brilliant,' I replied. My ears were ringing – a constant high-pitched tone cutting through my head.

'You liked the singer, did you?'

I didn't know what to say and made a complete hash of my reply. My mum just laughed. 'Don't worry. I know what young boys are like.'

I tried to change the subject. 'Robbo said they're close to making a record deal, with a proper producer.'

'Really?'

'He said when they go on tour, I can be a roadie.'

'Yeah.' She pulled open a taxi door, stepping aside to let me in. 'Robbo says a lot of things.'

•

By the end of the holidays I had developed a talent for drawing a perfectly curved female form. At least I thought they were perfect.

My mum caught sight of one. 'Twelve inch waist and thirty-eight inch boobs,' she said with a smile. 'Nice.'

'Very funny.' I moved the drawing aside, so she took

one of my fantasy art books and decided to pick on that instead.

'Don't you ever get fat Amazonians?'

'Hey, give that back.' I snatched at it, but she was too fast.

'Or even ones that wear clothes,' she added.

I tried again. This time I succeeded in grabbing the book but I lost the battle to hold back a laugh.

I pointed to the door. 'Out.'

•

Robbo left our house for the last time early one Sunday morning. I was downstairs watching TV and doodling when I heard him coming down the stairs. Not clumping down like he usually did; he was taking the stairs one at a time, hardly making any sound at all. When he stepped in the front room he had a holdall in his left hand and his boots in his right. He looked surprised to see me.

'Kyle,' he said. 'Hi.'

I looked at the bag in his hand. 'Where are you going?'

He put a finger to his lips, closed the door and started pulling on his boots.

'Just got a call,' he said, 'late last night.'

I sat up. 'From a producer?'

I never actually knew what a producer was, but Robbo used to talk about them all the time. He said that one day he'd get a call and that's when the money would come rolling in.

Robbo grinned, 'That's right, Kyle. A *top* producer. I've got to meet with the rest of the band, get things sorted out.'

I looked at the bag. It was stuffed full. Robbo followed my gaze.

'Er, yeah. The thing is, we've got to go down to London. That's where it all happens in the music biz.'

'Are you coming back?'

'Course I am. We're mates, aren't we?'

'And I'll still get to be a roadie?'

He put his finger to his lips again and glanced back at the door, and then in a lower voice he said, 'I'll make you my number one, Kyle. As soon as we get the dates for that first tour, I'll give you a ring.'

He finished lacing his boots, stood up and picked up his bag. 'See ya.'

It was an hour later before my mum came downstairs. She looked about the front room and said, 'He's gone then, has he?'

I wasn't quite sure what to say. I thought she'd know all about the call he'd got. 'He said he's going to London. With the band.'

Mum nodded.

'Sounds like good news,' I said.

She smiled with just the corner of her mouth. 'Well, he certainly got some news, but I don't know how good it was.' She came over and put her arms around me. 'I'm too independent, Kyle. That's my trouble. I like things my own way too much.'

And that's pretty much all she said on the subject.

One week later, she took me out for a pizza. That's when she told me there was going to be an addition to our family.

•

When I started back at school in September, Alex was there too. And he was in my class. He didn't have much of a sense of humour and rarely took part in group discussions. For the most part he kept his head down and got on with his work, but every now and then, his wide, grey eyes would flick about, watching, taking everything in.

Then he'd get back to work.

I tried not to give him a lot of thought in that first term. There was a baby coming and my mum wanted me to help out. She had a plan to decorate the spare room, to make it into a nursery.

And so we got started. I stripped the old paper from the walls pretty much by myself. When it came to the actual decorating, mum hung the new wallpaper, but I pasted it. She put the wardrobe together, but I read the instructions and told her what was what. She supported the shelves, but I held the cordless screwdriver and screwed the fixings.

As we decorated, we talked about names. She seemed to think the baby was going to be a girl and suggested things like Katie and Susan and Jennifer. But I knew it was going to be a boy and came up with decent names like Steve and Zac. Mum wasn't too keen. When I suggested Robbo she looked ready to swing for me.

The finished nursery looked stunning. The carpet had planes and trains and teddy bears on it. The wallpaper was sky blue with tiny white bunny rabbits. The wardrobe was all different colours – bright-green sides, orange doors, yellow handles and a blue top. The shelves were different colours too. Only the cot was a simple white with a musical mobile hanging over the top.

The work was done, and the nursery was finished. All that was missing was the baby, and by Christmas, my mum was looking big.

ALEX

For me, the cage fights came to an end on a cold Friday night in January.

Huge gas heaters that looked like jet engines were brought inside to keep the warehouse warm and people came in wearing big coats, hats and gloves, shaking each other by the hand and saying, 'All-the-best,' for the new year.

My opponent was a monster of a lad from Seaham. He was not only head and shoulders above me, but he had a lot more experience too. I should never have been put up against him. Everyone said so but the fight was to go ahead regardless.

My dad was brimming with confidence. 'You just do your best, Alex.' And for once, I saw him take a swig before the match had even started.

But as soon as I stepped inside the cage and the door locked, it was clear that I was out of my league.

I can't remember a lot about the fight other than pain

and confusion. The blows were coming out of nowhere, thick and fast. The other lad was doing all kinds of kung-fu and acrobatic moves. I couldn't get near him.

But then he made a mistake. He hit the deck and did a leg sweep, kicking my legs from under me. I went down, but not the way he'd intended. I fell on top of him and our heads smashed together.

I thought it was all over. I put a hand to the back of my head to stop the world spinning, climbed to my feet and felt for the cage for support.

Jim Banks was the MC that night. I could hear him counting, '... three, four ...' and looked to see my opponent lying flat out across the canvas.

'... nine ... ten! We have a winner.'

The cage door opened, and while a medic ran to the other lad, the MC grabbed my hand. 'Master Alex Crow.'

Boos rang out from the crowd, people were on their feet, there were shouts of 'Bollocks'.

I caught sight of my dad in the audience. He looked furious. Someone next to him yelled out, 'Knock-out! Alex won fair and square.' Someone else called out, 'Go on, Alex!'

A fight broke out. Tables went over, bottles smashed.

Jim Banks tried to call order but no one was listening. All he got was a barrage of abuse and a second fight broke out. Jim tried again, yelling into the mic for them to sit down. This time he managed to get their attention and announced that on account of the skills of both parties, the match was to be declared a draw.

If his intentions were to calm the place down, he'd certainly misjudged the crowd. If anything, it made things worse. Fans of my opponent were going wild, hailing him as the better fighter. Others were going mad because it was a knock-out, therefore a clear win. Screams came from the back of the room. A bottle flew through the air and smashed against the cage.

Jim turned the mic off, and put a hand on my shoulder. 'Sorry, son, this is getting ugly. Go and get yourself cleaned up.'

•

The toilets were pretty grim. There were no mirrors, just a single bog to piss in and a sink with a cold tap. Even so, it was a relief to get out of the main room, especially when the door closed, muffling the chaos out there.

My head was pounding. I checked with fingertips, carefully feeling the bump. Then I leaned forward and splashed water on my face, over my head and across the back of my neck.

When I straightened up, I realised it had gone quiet. A moment later, a loud cheer erupted. I paused and wondered what had happened to change things so radically. I decided I'd find out soon enough, cupped my hands under the tap and took a drink.

The door opened and Jim Banks walked in with a smile on his face.

'How you doing, kid?'

I was in a lot of pain but I managed, 'OK.'

'Sorry about the decision out there. If you'd been hailed the winner, you'd only regret it later. At least it's not marked down as a loss, eh?'

He stepped up to the bog, unzipped his fly and started to piss.

'Why were they cheering?' I asked.

'Oh that? Tensions were getting a bit high, so Joe told them it's free drinks for the next fifteen minutes. It's amazing what a drink can do.'

Another figure stepped into the toilets. I glanced round, surprised to see my dad standing there. He looked just as mad as before and he was staring at Jim with wide eyes. He had one hand in his pocket. He spotted me and stepped forward.

With his mouth right at my ear, he said, 'Get out.'

'I'm just . . .'

He kept his voice low and his eyes on Jim. 'Get out!'

'OK.'

I stepped away from the sink and shook my hands dry. That was when Jim realised that someone else was in the room with us, and assuming that my dad was waiting for the toilet he called over his shoulder, 'Just a sec.'

I had a feeling that my dad was going to have a go at him about the fight, but I was also worried because although Jim Banks was in his sixties, he had a bit of a history as a thug. Don't get me wrong, he was a friendly, decent bloke, but he still had that edge, a gritty undertone that told you he was no pushover.

I let the toilet door close behind me and stepped back into the main room. People were still angry about the outcome. I hoped I'd be able to get back to my seat without anyone giving me a hard time – I was certainly aware of people looking at me as I crossed the room.

I looked over my shoulder to see the toilet door open and my dad come out, walking fast. He caught up, grabbed me by the arm and said, 'Bar. Go to the bar.' He pushed me almost all the way there. The drinks were still free so he grabbed a bottle from the counter and took a good, long swig.

'What happened?' I asked. 'What did you say?'

His eyes flicked about and he leaned close. 'Keep your mouth shut. OK? When you came out of the bog, Jim was in there alone. You got that?'

'Why? What happened?'

He gripped my arm tight enough to hurt. 'He was alone.'

'I get it. I came out. Jim was alone. You didn't belt him, did you?'

'That bastard cost me three hundred quid.' He looked away and took another drink.

'Three hundred? You bet three hundred pounds?'

He shook his head. 'Jesus. I needed that money. I *really* needed that money.' Then he spat on the floor, cursing over and over.

I just stood there, stunned. I knew I had a knack for bringing down the bigger kids, but considering my opponent, that was one hell of a bet.

'How much would you have won?'

He looked up, slightly knocked by the question. Then he bit his lip and spat. 'The lower the odds, the more you need to put down.'

'But if it was a draw, surely, you can get that money back?'

He almost laughed. 'Shows what you know. You expect a draw, you bet on a draw. You expect a win, you bet on a win.'

'Why don't you say something to Joe?' I asked.

'Joe?' He looked at me like I had a screw loose. 'Joe?' he repeated. 'Joe couldn't give a toss who wins. Joe looks after Joe. He takes his money regardless. Joe never looses a damn penny. Why do you think he's dripping in gold?'

At that very moment, someone shouted for Joe. We both looked over. Some guy was standing by the bog door, holding onto the handle.

I looked at my dad. 'What happened?'

'Keep your mouth shut, boy. You understand me?'

His jacket was slightly open, and I could see something in his inside pocket; the lining was stretched and stained. From where I was standing, it just looked dark, but I knew if the lights were brighter, that stain would be red.

He saw me looking and closed his jacket.

The toilet door clattered and Joe came out. He went directly to the DJ stand, grabbed the microphone, knocked off the music and said, 'OK, folks, sorry to bring the evening to a close but I've just been informed that we've got a raid on our hands. There'll be a fleet of police vans here in about thirty seconds and they're looking to fill them all, so if you'd rather avoid a chat with the CID . . .'

The reaction was explosive. People grabbed jackets, bottles, cigarettes and ran for the exits.

My dad took another drink and stood his ground.

'Are we leaving too?' I asked.

He said nothing. Joe was walking this way.

My dad straightened himself up as Joe got near.

'A raid?' he said. 'You sure?'

Joe looked shaken. He glanced over his shoulder to check that everyone else was leaving, then he shook his head.

'We've got a problem.'

•

Jim Banks had been stabbed twice in the stomach and once in the throat.

Joe didn't care who had done it; he just wanted the body shifted.

There were seven blokes still in the warehouse – Joe, my dad, the bloke that found the body and four others. They all knew Jim, and were demanding that Joe find out who was responsible. Joe kept shushing them, but once they were sure that we were the only people left, they suddenly got louder and angrier. Finally, Joe snapped.

'Do you want a full investigation? Is that what you want? You want me to call the police right now, open this place up to the world, have our business spread over the local papers? Is that what you want? Because I'll tell you what, an unlicensed bar, gambling, cage fighting, that's more than enough to warrant a few arrests and the front cover of every local paper you can name, but *kids* fighting in cages! That'll make the national press. Is that what you want? You want your picture on the front of the *Star* and the *Sun* and the *Mirror*?'

The loudest of the men became suddenly sheepish and lowered his eyes. 'No, Joe. You know that's not what we want.'

'OK. OK. So now you're thinking. We all know that Jim had more than his fair share of enemies, and we think we know who was in here tonight, but face facts, boys, we don't exactly keep a register. Anyone could have got to him. It could have been down to his decision on the fight, or it could have been something that happened a month back. What we have here is a choice – to bring everything out in the open and share out the prison sentences, or shift the body and have it found elsewhere. Are we agreed?'

There was a mutter, then my dad spoke up, 'I guess you're talking sense.'

'But we still want to find out who did this,' added one of the others.

I bit my lip, then did my best not to.

'And we will,' said Joe. 'But we'll do it *our* way – without any help from the police or journalists or anything like that. Now, are we all agreed on what we need to do?'

'Where we gonna take him?'

Joe thought for a moment. 'Down by The Swan.'

'The Swan? It's all boarded up. So are half the buildings.'

'Precisely. It's out of the way. Quiet. No chance of witnesses, so just the sort of place you might go for a quiet deal.'

'Why don't we just chuck him in the river?' said one.

'Show some fuckin' respect, eh?' said another.

Joe continued. 'We want it to look like he was stabbed in the street, not hidden away or dumped in the river. If you do that, the first thing the police are going to do is try to track down where he *was* killed, and that might lead them here. So that's the plan. We take him down by The Swan, park his car and lie him close by. Agreed?'

Reluctant nods.

'Good.' He looked at me. 'Alex, there's a mop and bucket over by the bar. Go get it. Morris, go and line your boot with black bags.'

'Shouldn't we use Jim's car?'

'To move his body? Are you stupid? The first thing the police will do is have forensics turn that thing inside out – a drop of blood, a few skin cells and they'll know he'd been in the boot, which means he didn't die where they found him. But we do need his car there – and just as it is, with fag packets and all the crap he has lying on the passenger seat. The filthier the better. Harry, I want you to drive it. That means you keep well away from the toilet. Grab a bin liner, put it over the seat. You got gloves? No? Anyone got gloves for Harry? Good. Hand them over. The rest of you, come and help me shift the body.'

And so I was given the job of mopping the floor, cleaning all of the blood from around the bowl of the toilet, from the walls and the bog itself, while the others went off with the body – my dad included.

I looked down at the mess streaked across the floor. My head was still thumping and the more I thought about what was going on, the more it hurt.

I blinked hard, tried to think of the blood as paint. Spilt paint. Just something to be cleaned.

Mop. Rinse. Ring out.

Mop. Rinse. Ring out.

I got lost in the monotony. Time slipped away and when I eventually heard them coming back in, I had no idea how long they'd been.

My job was done. That was the main thing.

My dad's only words were, 'Let's go,' and he led me to the car. We drove home in silence, but as we pulled up at our house he turned to me and said, 'I don't want this mentioned. Not to your mam, not to anyone. You understand?'

'Yeah.'

'We'll talk about it tomorrow, yeah?'

'Yeah.'

And that was that.

I don't remember going to bed. I don't remember falling asleep.

·

I awoke the next morning to the clatter of the front door slamming shut. A second later the car started up.

My dad, leaving.

Where? The police?

No. Not the police. He'd never do that in a million years.

So where? It was dark outside. Still early. Too early to be going for a newspaper.

I waited in silence, waiting to hear if he came back. As I waited, I started to go over events from the night before. I began to feel angry, scared . . . even guilty. If I had just gone down, fallen a different way and lost the fight, there would have been no one to blame. Jim Banks would still be alive.

But instead, he was out there, outside in the cold and dark. As I lay in a comfortable, warm bed, Jim Banks was lying dead on a cracked, weed-ridden pavement by some boarded-up pub.

Was that where my dad was headed?

My dad – my own *dad* – had killed a man. Jim Banks, who had been alive and laughing and taking a piss right next to me, just a few hours ago, was dead. And my dad was the guy who stabbed him.

But that couldn't be right. Did that make him a murderer? Murderers were people that crept around at night hunting their victims. Murderers were evil, calculating monsters . . .

Not my dad. Not *my* dad.

Oh, yes it was, and you had to mop up the blood.

And then it hit me that I was wearing the same clothes from last night, the same clothes I'd fought in, the same clothes I'd stood in the toilet with mop in hand.

I got up, slung everything I had on in the wash basket and went straight to the bathroom. I stood in the bath with the shower on full, scrubbing my hands with soap, going over and over the same thoughts.

How long before Jim Banks was found? Who would find him? Someone walking their dog? A postman? A road sweeper. Had someone seen the cars last night? Had they seen Joe and my dad and the others carrying the body out of the boot and dumping it down on the pavement? Would they have realised what it was? How long until the police began rounding people up?

Suddenly, I could imagine hearing BANG, BANG, BANG on the door. Police bursting in, dragging me out of the bathroom, handcuffs. Down to the station in nothing more than a dressing gown. They'd quiz me night and day – good cop, bad cop – keep at me until I cracked, until I broke and gave evidence against my own dad.

Any second now. That's what would happen. I was certain of it.

I was wide awake, head thumping, pulse going crazy.

I had to get out.

I got dried, dressed and left the house.

I wandered around in the cold morning air. Dawn was breaking and there was a layer of ice on the ground. In the houses that I passed, people would have their heating on max. They were checking their mail, pouring milk on cereal, getting ready to face another ordinary day while I thought about the toilet, the body and the blood I had to mop up.

I got so worked up that I decided I was only avoiding the inevitable. I mean this *was* murder. And sooner or later, the police *would* track me down, drag me in and keep me there until I talked.

Suddenly, it was too much to bear. I just wanted it over and done with.

Worried, angry and confused, I actually stepped onto a bus that would take me to the police station.

But something happened at the bus stop. I got on board, but the bus didn't move off. I sat there, my eyes fixed on a point outside, waiting, trying my best not to think of what I was doing, where I was going, what I would say.

And still the bus didn't move.

I tried my best, I really did. I tried to keep my mind blank. Shut.

But in the end, time won. People around me were moaning and grumbling because the bus still didn't move.

And my thoughts, my fears, took over.

KYLE

I'll never forget the day Alex Crow snapped, not just because of what he did, but because I shouldn't have even been at school that day.

Sometimes, my mum had to work weekends. The second Saturday in January was one of those days. But she wasn't happy about it. The whole world was powdered with white frost and a fine, icy mist hung in the air.

'Why don't you call in sick?' I suggested.

'Because once you do that, you start to think it's OK to do it again. Besides, they'll never get anyone to fill in at such late notice.' She took another look through the window. 'Hat, coat, scarf and warm socks. No such thing as bad weather, Kyle. Just the wrong clothing.'

When she worked weekends she usually phoned home around dinner time. But on that day, the call came early.

'Kyle?'

Just one word, but her tone was enough to fire alarm bells. Something was wrong.

'Now, Kyle, don't get upset, OK? I'm in hospital, but I'm fine. You hear?'

'Hospital?'

'I'm in the maternity unit. I'll explain when you get here, so call a taxi. Don't get a bus. Just call a taxi, will you? I'll see you soon, pet.'

Oh shit.

I needed a taxi. I needed *money* for a taxi. Hell, I even needed a number for a taxi.

I rushed about the house in a whirl of panic. What was she doing in hospital? The baby wasn't due for . . . I had to think . . . March, wasn't it? That was another two months.

I found money, I found a number and I called a taxi rank.

Five minutes, they said. Five minutes. Not long.

I paced the floor, waiting. Back and forth, back and forth. Checked the clock.

Ten minutes had passed.

What was wrong? Where were they? Should I call again?

Finally, I heard a car pull up outside. Before it had a chance to honk its horn, I was out, locking the front door and then diving into the back seat. The driver knew where I was going. I expected him to shoot off with a roar of engine and a screech of tyres, but for some reason he seemed to drive slow, so painfully slow. I didn't have the guts to tell him to hurry, so instead I sat there, tapping a fingernail on the seat, my heart racing, my mind going over the same questions: what was my mum doing in hospital? Was the baby OK? Was my mum OK?

There were four beds in her room – all occupied. The other women were surrounded by cards and flowers and silver helium balloons with 'It's a boy' and 'A baby girl' printed on them and there were cots by the bedside. And these other women, they had visitors, all talking about the new baby, looking in the cot, asking for a hold while the mother unwrapped presents of woolly hats and knitted cardigans as music played on a radio.

There was no cot next to my mum. No baby. No cards.

There was a nurse by her side, talking to her, but I could tell from my mum's face that something was terribly wrong. Her skin was pale, her eyes were red from crying and her lips were dry and chapped.

She saw me hovering by the door and smiled. 'Kyle.' She held out her arms. 'Come here, love.'

I paused, still confused. 'What happened?'

The nurse moved to one side. 'So you're the big brother, are you?'

It took a second to make sense. 'The baby?'

My mum answered, 'He's upstairs. In the Special Care Unit.'

'He?' I asked. I should have been ecstatic but I just felt numb.

Mum nodded. 'He's a boy. You were right all along.'

'And he's doing fine,' said the nurse – although her words were more directed at my mum than me.

I looked again at the other cots, busy with blankets and baby toys. 'Why?'

'Because he's small.' She wiped her eyes with a tissue. 'He's just very small.'

'No, I mean . . . he's not due for ages.'

She nodded. 'It happened as I got off the bus.'

'What? What happened?'

There were more tears in her eyes. This time she tried to blink them away.

It was too much to bear. I felt tears in my own eyes. The only thing to do was to throw my arms around my mum. She hugged me back, but her hug was weak, and she released me with a gentle pat on my shoulder.

'It was an accident,' she said. 'Just a stupid, silly accident. I tried to step off the bus as someone else was getting on. I lost my footing and fell. The bus driver came straight out. He told me to keep still and called for an ambulance. Some of the passengers were grumbling, so he gave them a choice – sit and wait, or get off the bus and catch another. But he stayed with me until the ambulance turned up. Then I was on my way to hospital and straight to theatre.'

I paused before asking my next question. 'What about the baby?'

'The baby's fine. They'll take me across later to see him. I'm not really up to it right now.'

The nurse turned to face me. 'Tell you what, why don't I take *you* to see him? Your mum's just had an operation. She needs rest.'

My mum nodded, briefly closing her eyes.

'Go on, Kyle,' she said. 'Go and see your little brother.'

The nurse took me out of the ward and down a short corridor.

'It's not far,' she said. 'Just along here. We call it "Scabboo", from the initials.' She pointed to the sign above us – SCBU. 'Special Care Baby Unit. Scabboo for short.'

She stopped by a door and pointed to the intercom on the wall. 'I'll let you in, but when you come back, push the button, wait for someone to answer and tell them who you are. There's a little camera at the top so they can see you.'

She shielded the keypad with one hand, tapped in a code and the door unlocked.

•

As soon as I walked into the Special Care Baby Unit, I could see them – tiny little babies, some naked, some dressed – all lying in clear plastic incubators. There was no music in here, but there was plenty of sound – clicks and beeps of various monitors, the whisper of conversation, the hum of a fan and the occasional alarm. Down in the ward where my mum was, the place was full of parents' laughter and babies' cries, the smell of nappies and baby cream and talcum powder and fresh flowers. There were cards and balloons and presents. Not in here. In here, the surfaces were clean, the decorations were few and nurses noted down observations like assistants in a science lab.

The nurse caught my attention with a gentle hand. 'First things first,' she said. 'You need to scrub your hands. Come on, I'll show you the drill.'

There was a sink with a foul-smelling, bright-pink soap. I washed my hands, but the nurse shook her head.

'Like this,' she said, washing each and every finger, the backs of her hand, wrists, then interlocking fingers, front over back. Rinse, repeat.

I dried them on paper towels and she led me towards the nearest incubator.

A tiny, high-pitched mewling noise caused me to jump. On top of the incubator was a single card and next to it was a tiny, blue teddy bear. I cautiously approached, looked at the card and, without touching, I read, 'Happy Birthday, love from all the nurses in SCBU.'

The nurse was still by my side. 'That's him,' she said. 'That's your baby brother.'

I couldn't speak. He wasn't just small, he was *too* small. His head was no bigger than a tennis ball. The nappy he wore came right up over his chest. His hands were barely big enough to grip my little finger.

'He's tiny,' I said, stepping closer.

My baby brother lay on his front with his head turned towards me, his eyes tight shut. He was small, but he looked normal – I mean, he looked like a baby. He had the right number of fingers, the right number of toes, a whisper of hair. He was real, and he was alive.

But the weirdest thing was wanting to leave. Some of the other babies in the unit had visitors – probably parents – who sat by their incubator, looking in and smiling or chatting to the baby. I felt far too self conscious to try talking to a baby. He was asleep and I felt completely out of place.

So I did the only thing I could do. I went down to the shop in the hospital foyer, bought a couple of pencils and a pad of paper, and then I made my way back to the Special Care Baby Unit. I had to go through the cleaning routine again, but I soon settled down and started to draw. As carefully as I could, beginning with the faintest possible lines, I drew a picture of my baby brother as he slept.

I had been there over an hour and was only just finishing

when I heard a familiar voice say, 'Hello.'

My mum was in a wheelchair, being pushed by a porter.

I moved aside while a nurse took the baby out of his incubator and placed him gently in my mum's arms. Tears were rolling down her face as she fed him, changed his nappy and dressed him in clothes that wouldn't fit a doll.

'Have you got a name for him yet?' the nurse asked.

My mum looked at the baby. 'Christopher,' she said. She looked at me. 'If that's OK with you.'

It seemed to come out of nowhere. It wasn't a name either of us had mentioned before, but now that he was here, lying in her arms . . .

'It's perfect,' I said.

She was over the moon about my drawing. She said she'd take it back to the ward with her, have it pinned above her bed so that she, like the other mothers in the room, could see her baby whenever she wanted.

I had a moment of panic when my gran turned up and suggested I stay at her house while my mum was in hospital. Once I realised there was no chance of them letting me stay home alone, I argued an alternative. I mentioned school and homework – that it would make more sense for *her* to come home with *me*. Gran wasn't happy, but Mum agreed.

I breathed a sigh of relief. At least I would be able to escape to my room.

•

I went to the hospital twice the next day. At first, everything was fine, but in the afternoon, during a feed, an alarm kept going off. The nurse just silenced it at first, checked on Christopher and gave us reassurance. But when Christopher started to look grey she lost her smile and called for help.

Nurses and doctors appeared from nowhere. I was moved aside, the baby was taken from my mum and she was wheeled backwards, out of the way. Christopher's incubator was suddenly surrounded by people and equipment.

Christopher was put on a machine to help him breathe. When they finally settled him down and I got another look at him, I noticed several new tubes attached to his hands and feet. His face had returned to a more healthy pink, the monitors had stopped alarming and Christopher was asleep on his back, his tiny chest moving in time to the hiss of the ventilator.

I felt sick, but I hung about – I've no idea how long – just until I was satisfied those alarms weren't going to kick off again.

'I think he's going to be all right,' my mum whispered. But she was watching the monitors more than the baby.

'I'll come back tomorrow, after school.'

With a tired smile, she said, 'You can stay off school if you want. I'll give them a ring, explain what's going on with the baby. You can come back here in the morning.'

But I made an excuse and opted for school.

•

So there I was, in class.

The first lesson of the day was maths, and the teacher, Mr Slate, was one of the strictest, meanest teachers in the school.

Most people were already seated. As Mr Slate began writing stuff on the board, Alex wandered in late. He walked past his regular seat and kept on going towards the back of the class. He stopped by a boy called David McKenzie, who was sitting where he always sat – right at the back, near the window.

'You're in my seat.'

McKenzie actually laughed. 'What are you talking about?'

But Alex didn't smile. 'That's my seat, McKenzie. Move.'

'Get your own damn seat.'

Wham! Alex punched him on the side of the head and dragged him out of his chair. As David fell on the floor, Alex stepped over him, sat down and swiped a hand across the desk, knocking books, pens and everything else onto the floor with David. This all happened before Mr Slate finished writing and turned to face the class.

'What's going on back there?'

Alex replied, 'David fell over, sir.'

Slate glared at the boy on the floor and demanded, 'So why are you still sitting there?'

Alex whispered something as David got to his feet, and David looked visibly shaken. He looked at the teacher and mumbled, 'I was just getting up, sir.'

Slate bellowed, 'Find a seat and settle down. We have not got all day. The rest of you, get your work books open at page sixty-two. On the menu for today – transposition of formulae. Jones, sit up straight. Cook, read the question out loud.'

Alex, who usually excelled in maths, sat in his new seat and stared out of the window. He opened his books, I saw him look at them once or twice, but I don't think he put pen to paper all lesson.

At break time, he started on someone else and I heard from Gareth that he did the same thing in the afternoon, but by that time I was out of there. Straight after morning break I was told to go to the secretary's office.

Gran was waiting there for me. My mum wanted me back at the hospital.

•

It took me a long, long time to get over the death of my little brother.

He didn't die on the day I was taken out of school; my mum just needed me there.

He hung on for another three days. Torturously long for us, but far too short and painfully unfair for Christopher.

I spent most of that time at the hospital, listening to the doctors speak in words I couldn't understand, hoping that things would change, wondering why they weren't doing more.

And I was there when my mum dressed him for the last time, listened to the chaplain baptise him, and sat with her during Christopher's final hour of life.

We had to say goodbye, and his ventilator was quietly turned off.

ALEX

Jim Banks's body was found around the time I stepped off that bus. The story hit the local news at six o'clock. By which time, I was back home.

I'd spent the day wandering here there and everywhere, lost in a paranoid world, with the police one side and the gangsters and local villains from the warehouse on the other.

When I returned home, my mum was right on cue with tea, serving me a plate of egg, chips, beans and four greasy sausages.

I mumbled, 'I'm not that hungry.'

'Aren't you?' she looked at me. 'You don't look too well.' She adjusted the plate, as though it wasn't close enough. 'A good meal will probably do you the world of good.'

I looked down at the dry, lukewarm beans, the split egg, the swimming grease. I stabbed my fork into a sausage and took a small bite.

That was when the story hit.

My dad was sitting in that same old armchair, one hand scratching his stubble, eyes never leaving the TV.

The details were few. No footage of the area, no name given. Just a report that police were appealing for witnesses after a man, thought to be in his sixties, was found dead with knife wounds.

'Oh, would you listen to that?' said my mam. 'You're afraid to leave the house these days. Where did they say it was?'

I couldn't help myself. 'The Swan, wasn't it?'

My dad flicked his eyes towards me. He knew for a fact that the name of the pub hadn't been mentioned. 'Somewhere like that.'

My mam hadn't caught on, and merely said, 'It's terrible.'

'Rough area,' said my dad. 'Probably drugs related. Dealing on the wrong patch.'

'What,' my mam said. 'In his sixties?'

'Oh, aye. The kids down there don't care. Probably mugged him first.'

I got up. I couldn't bear to be in the same room.

•

The next day was Sunday, which was normally a day for the club, training with Carlos. I was going three times a week at that point, but that day I knew before I got out of bed that I couldn't face it. They'd all be talking about Jim Banks. He'd been a regular MC, so we all knew him well. On top of that, they'd want to hear about the fight, how it had ended in a draw, if I thought that had anything to do with Jim being found dead the next day.

But it went deeper than that. Even the thought of the cage itself made me uncomfortable, and once again I was left thinking that the whole thing was somehow my fault.

'Not off to boxing?' my mam asked, working her way through a pile of ironing while I was slumped on the sofa. She always called it boxing. She had no idea what I really did over there.

I replied with a simple, 'No.'

I was waiting for my dad to say something – *willing* him to say something – but he just sat there, stuck in his chair, reading his newspaper in silence.

I stared at him, hardly able to believe I was sitting in my front room with a murderer.

My aunty Pat's got this saying: 'See his fatha's eyes.' It's one of those things that reminds you she wasn't always posh, a throwback saying from years ago that she only ever delivers in a broad, Wearside accent. She'd say it about Neil whenever he did something good, especially when it was something that Uncle Joe would be proud of. It meant that she could see Joe in her son's eyes – it was a way of saying he'd grow up to be like his dad.

I kept staring, and I knew that he knew I was staring. Good. Because that's what I wanted. Any second now, he'd slap down his paper and snap, 'What you gawpin' at, boy?' and then he'd shoot to his feet, his face red, his teeth clenched, a fist ready to crack me for staring at him like that. And then I'd be on my feet too, ready to block his strike and hit him back, and my mam, still ironing, would see us laying into each other, and she'd laugh and pat her chest as though she was watching the cutest little puppy and say, 'Oh, look at that. See his fatha's eyes.'

And then I'd know. I'd know that I could be a murderer too.

But that never happened. My dad knew I was watching him and he just stared all the harder at his paper.

Eventually I'd had enough. I got up and left.

•

That night, I kept thinking of all the things I could say to him, of all the things I *should* say to him. Because I needed to get this whole thing out in the open, to find out what he planned to do, to find out if he was ever going to get caught.

But even if I'd had the guts to say something, by the time I got up on Monday morning, he'd already left the house.

I guess that's what made me snap when I got to school.

I started with David McKenzie, cracking him on the head and dragging him from his seat. I didn't care that the teacher was in the room, or that the teacher in question was Slate. All the better, in fact. I expected to get caught, for Slate to lose his rag, drag me to the headmaster's office where they'd put me over the coals, threaten to expel me and I'd end up spilling the whole thing about my dad and the cage fights and the murder. It would all come out. Everything.

But that didn't happen. Slate just told us to get on with our work.

So at break time I cracked someone else, at dinner time I kicked the shit out of another. That fight got broken up, but the teacher just wrote me up for detention. I actually laughed as I walked off.

At home time, some kid pushed past me to get through the gates. I grabbed him, pulled him round and pinned him to the iron railings.

Then I saw the fear in his eyes. He was a year older than me, and not exactly a nerd, but he knew he was going to get laced.

It was pathetic. This wasn't fighting. Real fighting needed a half decent opponent.

There's a time for fighting. A time and a place.

Oh yeah, I knew all about that now. The smell of sweat, of cigarettes and beer, the clash of a steel door, the cheer of a crowd, the thrill of being a real winner.

I let the kid go.

The next day, the same thing happened again. I had every intention of leathering someone just for looking at me, but when it came to it, when his hands went up to protect his face and he cried out in fear, I ended up walking away.

I put the school fights aside but I couldn't concentrate on work. Every time I got my head down, I'd end up thinking about the cage and the warehouse. And that would get me thinking of the toilet, wringing out the mop with my bare hands, watching the blood swirl and wash down the drain.

My work slipped, and it was that, not the fighting that won me my next detention. And that was fine by me. The thought of going home to sit in the same house as my father made me feel physically sick. So I made sure the detentions became a regular event.

But detention only ever lasted an hour – more often a lot less, and at home, time seemed to tick slower and slower.

The police never did come knocking. The news of the murder had been reported in the local papers just as my dad had said – a drug-related killing. It was a bad area, and the story was soon forgotten. Perhaps the police didn't feel the need to investigate these things. I don't know. All I did know was the weeks went by. My dad was permanently on edge, jumping every time the postman rattled the letterbox.

And my mam began to develop bruises.

KYLE

The months that followed Christopher's death were horrible. At home, we tried to go about things as though everything was the same. My mum would drift off now and then and I found myself doing the same at school. Even weeks later it would hit me, taking me totally off guard, that my brother was gone. There was no baby.

But life went on. I spent dinner and break times with Gareth and Jamie Spencer. We had a regular game of throwing insults at each other – the best ones involving sex or the size of our equipment. They covered for me for a while, but gradually, I fell back into my old stride.

'My dick is so big I've got to wrap it round my waist.'

'I have to wheel mine round in a barrow.'

'Yeah, right. Yours is so small you think you've got three knackers.'

'Oh yeah? Well if yours was any shorter, you'd be a girl.'

'You *are* a girl!'

'So how come I shagged your mum?'

'Because his mum's a lezzer.'

And so on, and so on.

But not everyone appreciates a clown. Alex Crow, for example. Ever since the Christmas break, he always seemed angry. His random attacks were short-lived, but he always seemed ready to snap. He had taken to wandering the schoolyard, rather than sitting alone. And more often than not, he wandered next to us. When he did, we would put our jokes and insults to one side, each of us worried that one word out of turn could result in Alex snapping and beating any one – or even *all* – of us senseless.

But when you make jokes day in day out, it becomes second nature. And sometimes it's hard to turn off.

It was only a matter of time before I let my guard down and something slipped.

ALEX

I hated the idea that my dad was taking his frustrations out on my mam. Hated it. I wanted to do something, say something, I really did. But how do you pick the right moment?

So when the bruises began to yellow and fade, and weren't replaced, I thought maybe he was calming down. He still hounded her, he still turned the slightest thing into an argument, but instead of lashing out he'd hit a wall, or swear or give her a torrent of verbal abuse.

He wasn't calming down. He was just changing tactics.

I soon realised why.

It was just a normal boring evening. I was on one end of the sofa, my mam was on the other and my dad was in his armchair. Right in the middle of whatever we were watching, he spoke up.

'Going to be a good fight tomorrow night.'

It came totally out of the blue. And it wasn't even like he

was saying it to me, just speaking out in general.

When I didn't respond, he shuffled his seating and added, 'I'm talking about the adults, of course. The juniors aren't up to much these days. Last few fights have been disappointing. Joe was saying that very thing, just last week.' He was surprisingly cool about it. He didn't sound like himself at all.

I felt like replying, 'What do you care?' but the mention of Joe caught my attention.

My dad noticed and shrugged. 'That's what he said. He seems to think you're something special. It would be good, you know, to see you back in there.'

By 'there', he meant the cage. I thought this over for a second. Then I asked, 'Is that what *you* think?'

He seemed to get narked by the question, looking like he'd wished he'd never bothered to say anything and snapped, 'You win your fights, don't you?'

I suppose I was lucky to get that much from him.

I turned my attention back to the TV.

After a few minutes, my dad cleared his throat. 'So are you coming, or what?'

'Coming where?' And yeah, I knew what he was asking. I just wanted to hear him spell it out.

'Coming to the fight. Joe'll be there.'

My mam suddenly spoke up, 'You used to be dead keen on your boxing.'

I felt a spark of guilt that she was still under the illusion that the fights were all above board and took place in a working men's club – not some rundown warehouse in the middle of nowhere.

Guilt was overpowered with anger. Of course I wanted to

go back. I wanted to see the cage. See the fighters – the adults *and* the kids. I wanted it all back, but that's not why I was angry. I was angry with myself. I felt as though one mention of the cage fights should bring back all the horror of that night. The stain on the inside of my dad's jacket, the mop and the blood and the sink. I should have been disgusted at the very idea of going back. But instead, I felt like I was hacking off my nose to spite my face. Instead, it all seemed so long ago, not just a month or two.

I missed the cage. There was no doubt about that. I missed it all, and beating up losers at school was a piss poor substitute. That was why every fibre in my body was yelling out, 'It's over! It's OK to go back!' The investigation into Jim's murder was filed and forgotten. The toilet had been cleaned and used and cleaned again – too many times to even care about. It was over. But the fights were going on, week in, week out, and I was missing every one.

It seemed like my reason not to go wasn't as strong as it should have been. That's why I was angry. And that's why I was disgusted in myself.

So instead, I relied on something Neil had said to me. 'Juniors can't just turn up,' I said. 'If you're not going in the cage, then you're not invited.'

'That's a guideline,' said my dad. 'Not a rule. Joe would like to see you back. Said so himself. He said he needs someone to show these other kids how it *should* be done.'

I found myself biting the side of my thumb. It took everything I had to say, 'No.'

'Well,' said my mam. 'You'll see your uncle Joe in two weeks time, won't you?'

This took me by surprise. 'Will I? What for?'

'Neil's birthday.'

My blank expression prompted her to add, 'The invite's been on the fridge for weeks.'

The penny dropped. Neil's seventeenth. They were planning some big family bash.

I felt like kicking myself. How could I have been so blind? That explained my dad's change towards my mam – hitting the wall instead of her arms, head, face.

But it didn't explain him talking about the fights.

Once again, I felt like asking him, 'What do you care?' Because it bothered me. He was never particularly proud of me. All he cared about were his bets.

So why did he suddenly want me back in that cage?

•

Neil's birthday celebrations were held in a room in one of Joe's city centre nightclubs. We got the bus there, mainly because my dad wanted a few drinks and my mam – well, she'd already had a few.

While my dad sat straight, keeping his eyes on the road ahead through the huge bus windscreen, my mam looked relaxed and quite excited. I was sitting sideways on the seat behind them. Every now and then she'd turn to say things like, 'It'll be good to see the family all together again.'

It was nice to hear her so upbeat. It was also good to see her completely free of all those knocks, scratches or other 'accidents' that left their little hallmarks, but knowing how much of a struggle it was for my dad to hold back made me wish she'd had a genuine accident, just to give her something for Aunty Pat to ask about. As the bus went past the houses, the cemetery and the hospital, I found myself lost in a fantasy conversation, telling my aunty, 'She's always got bruises. Every time they have an argument.'

My mam broke my thoughts. 'It's years since I've been to a nightclub.'

'We're not going to a nightclub,' said my dad, still staring ahead. 'It's being held *in* a nightclub, but we're not going *to* a nightclub, are we?'

'What's the difference?' I said, feeling yet another argument about nothing coming up.

'Because Neil couldn't legally get in, could he? On his seventeenth? Joe's not that daft. It's a private party. Not a nightclub.'

My mam shook her head, smiling. 'It's still a nightclub. There'll still be drink.'

'It's behind closed doors, you daft cow. A private party means a *private* party. Jesus, woman. What planet are you on?'

I was aware of other people on the bus looking our way.

My mam, oblivious to this, turned to me and said, 'Well, it's still been years since I've been to a nightclub. It'll be nice to see what a modern club is like these days.'

•

This particular club was below street level and quite small. There were two well dressed bouncers on the door who greeted us with short nods as we walked inside. The corridor split at a T-junction with double doors left and right. To the right there was a large sign with: 'PRIVATE PARTY. INVITATION ONLY'.

I glanced the other way and asked, 'So what's going on through there?'

'Nothing yet,' said my dad, checking his hair in the huge, wall-length mirror. 'Not for another hour or two. Nightclubs don't usually open until late. That's why they're called *night*clubs, isn't it?'

The room we walked into was small but complicated, with a dance floor at an even lower lever, walkways and seating around, snugs and enclosed areas, plus three small bars serving drinks. There was a DJ stand at the far side and music was playing, but the main lights were on and everyone seemed to be heading towards the same corner of the room.

It had only been a couple of months since I'd last seen Neil, but it took a second or two to recognise him. I'd never seen him dressed in anything other than ripped and tattered T-shirts, knee-length shorts or combats and lethal laced-up boots. This Neil seemed worlds apart. Older. Taller. He wore straight black trousers and a dress shirt, his hair was waxed and tidy and as I got closer I could see that his spots were almost all but cleared up.

'Alex,' he said, offering a hand. 'Wondered if you'd turn up.'

'Happy Birthday, Neil.'

He nodded. 'Yeah, and . . . ?'

'And what?'

His face was suddenly cold. 'Where's my present, maggot?'

'Present?' My mam had made me sign a card, but she never said anything about spending money on a . . .

'If you don't have a present, you can go straight back outside.'

He pushed his lower jaw forward, twisting his mouth in

utter disgust, and for a moment he had me. Then his grimace switched to a grin and a quick wink. 'Gotcha.' He flashed out a hand to cuff the side of my face. Without thinking, I blocked, gripped and twisted his arm aside.

'Whoa,' he laughed, snapping his hand away. 'Still got the magic, have you?'

'Never left me,' I said.

Another voice, deep, powerful and unmistakable came from my right. 'So why are you such a stranger all of a sudden?'

Before I got a chance to collect my thoughts, Uncle Joe clapped me on the back. 'Nice to see you, Alex. You've missed some good matches. Quite a few you could have won. What's up, you retired, or just having a break?' His face was a beaming smile, but I felt uncomfortable at the way he was watching me.

A quick glance at my dad was enough to confirm he was listening to every word. I tried to come up with something innocent, starting, 'I was just . . .'

'Don't worry about it,' Joe cut in. 'It does a lad good to have a break. Gives you some perspective. Isn't that right, Will?'

My dad grunted something behind a smile then quickly changed the subject. 'What you drinking, Joe?'

The room soon filled up, the lights went down and the music became louder. I met strangers who introduced themselves as family, I avoided the dance floor, had enough coke to make myself feel sick and ate more than I wanted when the buffet was finally opened. All the same, later in the night, I wandered back over to grab one of the remaining chicken drumsticks.

I leaned against the table and took a look about at the party. I saw my aunty Pat trying to drag my mam towards the dance floor. My mam laughed, shook her head and sat back down. My dad appeared to spend most of his time sitting forward, elbows on his knees, picking at the label on his beer bottle while he watched everyone else having a good time.

Neil was by the bar with his own group of friends – I'd tried chatting to them earlier, but was generally ignored as they knocked back tequila slammers and argued about football.

Aunty Pat gave up on my mam and went back to dancing with a circle of women in the middle of the dance floor. The whole lot of them were swaying and moving their arms like they hadn't a clue what song they were dancing to, but it didn't seem to bother any of them. They were laughing and nudging each other, hitching up their shoulder straps, occasionally daring something racy. All very embarrassing of course, but it also made me a little sad. Aunty Pat had loads of friends. Some were family from her side, but others were definitely friends. I could tell. There were a whole bunch of them. Whereas with my own mam, other than the odd neighbour who she'd chat to over the fence, she didn't have anyone she could go out dancing with. No one she could bring to a party like this. In fact, no real friends at all.

Then again, neither did I. Not really.

'Now there's a man deep in thought.'

I looked round, surprised to see Joe standing next to me.

'Finishing off the grub, are you? Not a bad idea. I think I might join you.'

He grabbed a slice of corned beef pie and motioned towards the seats. 'Have a sit down, Alex. Never looks good to be hovering around food.'

He followed me over, and as he sat, he put almost the whole slice of cold, greasy pie in his mouth. I felt a little uncomfortable and picked at the rest of my chicken.

'So what's on your mind?' he asked. 'Has seeing Neil over there got you thinking about the club?'

I shrugged. I didn't really know what to say.

Joe ate the rest of his slice and wiped his hands. 'I see your old man down at the warehouse every week. I've been asking him what's going on. Have you two had a falling out, or are you just growing tired of things?'

The music was loud in that room, and on my first attempt at answering, Joe leaned forward and asked me to repeat.

'I don't know. I just thought I'd take it easy for a while.'

Joe nodded, like he understood.

He didn't, of course. He had no idea.

But then he leaned towards me again and said, 'You know, Alex. All of that business with Jim Banks; it wasn't something a boy of your age should have seen. What we had there was a tricky situation. The important thing is that we dealt with it, and we sorted it out. We kept it under wraps. Do you understand what I'm saying, son? We kept it under *control*. That's an important word, Alex. I'm sure Carlos has spoken many times about maintaining control, hasn't he. You lose that, you lose the fight. Now, I'm going to say something important. And I want you to understand. OK?'

I nodded, feeling quite nervous about the whole conversation.

'It was wrong to make you help out that night. I'm glad that you *did* help out. You did a real good job. But you shouldn't have had to. You understand that? I'm sure it knocked

99

the stuffing out of you. Hell of a thing to see. And I can totally understand why you'd want to forget the whole ugly incident. And I can respect that too. Thing is, I get so many people, even the adult fighters, that keep saying, "Joe. When is that kid coming back?" They even know your name, saying, "When's Alex Crow fighting again?" going on and on about how good you were, how good you're going to be. So I could do with a little help here. I'd like to tell them whether or not you *are* coming back. I mean, in your own time, of course.'

I shrugged. Words just wouldn't come.

'Because,' added Joe, subtly looking about, 'that thing with Jim Banks. It wasn't anything to do with you. Not really. I mean, it's not like you saw anything, is it?'

I suddenly looked up to see Joe staring right at me.

Bollocks, I thought. *I lost my cool. I should have kept my eyes down.*

'See anything?' I asked, sounding as innocent as I could.

'I think you know what I mean, don't you?'

I tried to keep calm, to keep cool. But this was different to being in the cage and my heart was suddenly pounding like a drum. When I tried to speak up, I stammered.

A sudden change in music covered up for me, and Joe continued, 'Because if you did . . . Jim was a good friend. We go – went – way back, and I know he's got a few enemies hiding in the woodwork, but he's got a lot of friends too. Good friends. Friends that would make sure anyone who helped get to the bottom of this would stay safe. What I'm saying, Alex, is that if you *did* see something, you don't need to keep it bottled up.'

'I didn't,' I managed.

'But if you did. Just on the off chance. You'd have nothing to worry about should you . . . you know . . . mention it. To me.'

I glanced over towards the seats where my mam and dad were sitting. A couple of women were next to them, chatting. My dad was saying something, pointing, making a joke, my mam and the other women were laughing.

'I didn't see anything,' I said and got to my feet. 'Sorry, Uncle Joe. I didn't see a thing.'

Joe sat back and nodded. 'OK. Fine. I just thought I'd mention it. But if you ever want to go back to the club, I'm sure Carlos will be glad to see you.'

I nodded and moved away. As I walked through the nightclub, my eyes were back on my dad. Because now it made sense. Now I knew exactly why he wanted me back in that cage, and it was nothing to do with bets or fighting. He was worried. He was worried because Joe had been asking questions.

And yet, there he was, finally relaxing. Enjoying himself with friends and family like everything was fine and dandy.

And here I was, walking away from the perfect opportunity to speak up.

What was I doing? Why was I protecting him? Because he was my dad? Because that's what you did? Or because I was scared? Was it as simple as that? Was I just too soft to speak up?

I'm telling you, if there was a hole deep enough, I would have thrown myself in it right there. If I'd had a place to run, I would have legged it so fast that my feet wouldn't touch the ground. I felt like kicking something, breaking something, and I was biting the inside of my lip so hard that I could taste blood.

Sooner or later, I was going to explode.

KYLE

It happened a few weeks into the summer term, a time when breaks seemed too short and the lessons far too long. The classrooms got hot and sticky and the teacher's voice seemed to send us all to sleep. Sometimes, it was only the distant drone of a plane that told us there was still a world outside. During those days, the summer holidays seemed impossibly far away. We struggled through with moans and jokes and sarcasm – but I guess some people don't share my sense of humour.

It was our last lesson of the day – maths, with Mr Slate. He'd been pacing up and down the room in his standard fashion, his expression as serious as ever, waiting for us to complete the example he'd set.

He turned, picked someone at random and said, 'Well?'

'Thirty-two degrees,' came the reply.

Slate gave nothing away. His eyes settled on a girl at the

lurted out, 'Thirty-two,' without even

gaze on Gareth. I took a quick glance
orty-one'.
ish. 'Thirty-two.'

I couldn't help grinning. I gave him a nudge and nodded towards his book.

Gareth scowled at me and mouthed, 'Shut up!'

Luckily, Slate didn't see any of this. He was already searching for his next victim.

'Crow, what did you get?'

Alex was sitting in the chair he'd claimed from David McKenzie in January. He was leaning backwards and staring out of the window.

All eyes flicked from Alex back to Slate as he bellowed again, 'Crow!'

Alex snapped his head round. 'What?'

'I asked you a question, boy.'

'Yeah, well I'm thinking, aren't I?'

I could see Slate smouldering, but he didn't blow his top. Instead, he sat against the front of his desk and said, 'By that, I assume you have not done the exercise.'

'What exercise?'

'The one on the board. The one you should have been working on for the past ten minutes.'

Alex rolled his eyes and looked back out of the window.

'Crow! Are you going to give me an answer?'

'Er . . . thirty-two – the same as him.'

'Then you're a fool, Crow. The point of doing an exercise is not to get the correct answer; it is to understand *why* you get the correct answer.' He turned his attention to the rest of us. 'But thirty-two degrees *is* correct. So, assuming you are all expert in trigonometry, you can spend the rest of the lesson on the following worksheet.' He held up a pile of papers. 'Ten questions. Nothing taxing, so I don't expect anyone to get any wrong. Wrong answers will be dealt with in the usual manner.'

We all knew very well what 'the usual manner' was. We called it *The Walk of Shame*, and it meant going up to Slate's desk to pick up additional worksheets – five questions per sheet; one sheet for each wrong answer. It was evil, but it worked. Slate had the best pass results in the region.

He dropped the papers on my desk. 'Kyle, you win the honour of handing them out.'

It wasn't a task I relished, but neither would I argue. As Slate returned to his desk, I started handing out the papers, but when I got to Alex, I dropped two papers instead of one. It was a genuine mistake.

Alex, without malice, simply said, 'Here, one's enough.'

Cue my death-wish . . .

'You sure?' I said. 'It'll save you a walk later.'

Two seats away, Gareth snorted a laugh, and I realised with horror what I'd done.

Alex twisted round. 'What did you say?'

Oh shit.

I pretended not to hear and continued walking. Alex's hand shot out, grabbed my wrist and pulled me close.

'You think you're funny? Do you? Eh?'

I held up my free hand in mock surprise.

Alex snapped at Gareth, 'And you? You think he's funny?'

Slate looked up. 'What's going on down there?'

Alex released me, and it was up to me to say, 'Nothing, sir.'

'I heard raised voices.'

'I gave Alex two papers by mistake.'

A smile actually broke on Slate's lips. 'Then he should be thanking you. It will save him a walk later.'

The class erupted in laughter. And, thanks to me, all of that laughter was directed at Alex Crow.

As soon as Slate turned away, Alex shot me a look of pure hatred. 'When that bell goes, you're dead.' He pointed a finger at Gareth. 'That goes for you too, fat boy.'

I couldn't do a thing on that worksheet. I couldn't concentrate. I could *feel* Alex staring at me. I felt sick. Somehow I had managed to humiliate the school lunatic. What had I been thinking? How the hell was I going to stand up to someone like Alex Crow?

The answer was simple – I wasn't. I was going to die.

I checked my watch every few seconds. As the lesson neared its end I began sneaking my pen, calculator and other bits and pieces into my bag, quietly zipping it up, getting ready for the off. Gareth caught on and did the same. When the lesson was over we were going to have to run for our lives.

And then the bell rang.

In any other class we would all be up and out of the door, but this was Slate's lesson, and no one got up without his say-so. But instead of his usual, 'You may leave,' he looked towards the back of the room. 'Alex Crow, stay behind. I'd like a word with you.'

I looked at Gareth, who was clearly as shocked as I was. We couldn't believe our luck.

The corridors were full of kids heading for the exits, but

before we followed them outside, something occurred to me. I grabbed Gareth by the arm and pulled him towards the stairs. 'Quick. This way.'

'What? Why?'

'I'll tell you when we get there. Come on.'

He followed me to the foot of the stairs. We had to fight our way through the mass of bodies trying to descend, getting pushed this way and that, shouldered and jostled, but we made it and once we got to the top I ran towards the biology rooms.

'What are we doing up here?'

'Surviving.'

There was a hiding space near the technician's room where we could look out of the window and see the flow of kids being released from the school.

I leaned back against the wall. 'Slate isn't going to keep Alex very long, is he? And he can run faster than either of us. Plus, the bus isn't due for another five minutes, so he'll catch us at the bus stop anyway.' Alex got the same bus as we did. He got off at a later stop, but if he couldn't get us before the bus turned up, I had a good idea he'd make an exception and we'd find him stepping off a few stops early. Just to spend a little more time with us.

I looked down and saw Alex running towards the gates. 'Look. There he is. Slate couldn't have said more than five words to him.'

We watched as Alex reached the gates. He stopped there, looked about, searching for us. A moment later, he spat on the ground and leaned up against the railings.

'What's he doing?' asked Gareth.

'I think he's waiting for us. He knows we couldn't have beaten him.'

'So we wait until he gets on the bus?'

I shook my head. 'I don't think he's going to bother. He's just standing there.'

'Oh great. So what do we do now?'

I thought for a moment. 'We go the long way home.'

'What?'

'Over the sports field. There's a gap in the fence. We can go cross country.'

Gareth looked horrified. 'But that's miles.'

I could understand his worry. It wasn't exactly a short walk.

'It's better than getting beaten to a pulp,' I told him. 'Besides, if he doesn't see us, we can take it easy. It's not *that* far.'

Gareth took a few seconds to consider the options, but in the end he nodded and we set off.

We got to the sports field without incident and headed for the gap in the fence. This wasn't just a matter of one or two planks missing; a whole section had been ripped down. As we clambered over, I looked back to see if Alex was still waiting at the gates.

He was gone.

For a brief moment I almost relaxed, thinking he'd given up, gone home, but something over to the right – way past the football pitch – caught my eye.

It was Alex; he was keeping to the perimeter and he was running.

My mouth went dry. 'Leg it!'

And we did. We ran. Fear kept us focussed, an adrenalin overdose kept our legs working, kept us pushing, grunting, sweating, panting, running over wasteland, jumping or leaping to avoid broken bottles and dog shit, running for our lives, running to keep ahead of Alex Crow.

We made it to the viaduct – a huge stone railway bridge spanning the river. There was no danger of trains coming after us since the tracks that stretched out ahead of us were all rusted, forgotten and dotted with weeds. Over the far side, the land sloped up and up towards Penshaw Hill. There's an old monument right at the top – a monstrous thing with gigantic stone pillars and triangular, open roof, looking like some ancient Greek temple. Whenever I see it, I know I'm almost home.

But for Gareth, it was still too far.

We were halfway across that viaduct when I became aware that he was no longer by my side. I skidded to a halt to see what was going on and I saw that he hadn't just slowed down, he had stopped.

His whole face was bright red and soaked with sweat. He looked ready to faint, bent over, resting his hands on his knees. In that instant, the threat of Alex Crow was obliterated by another, greater fear.

•

Gareth hated PE, especially circuit training. We both did.

Our PE teacher was a big, mean old bastard called Briggs. While other PE teachers would have their favourite star pupils and put most of their effort into them, Briggs thought *everyone* should give one hundred per cent, all of the time. No excuses. No exceptions. So one day, when he saw Gareth lying flat on his back in the sit-ups zone, he nearly blew a gasket.

'Up,' he cried, striding over.

Gareth was red-faced, his eyes closed.

'Up. Now,' Briggs bellowed, standing over Gareth. 'A boy of your age should be able to do at least five circuits. You aren't even trying. Now come on!' He checked his watch. 'You've got another thirty seconds. I want to see at least, *at least*, two more.'

But Gareth didn't move so Briggs bent down, grabbed him by his top and heaved him up to a sitting position.

'One!' he called out.

Gareth slumped back to the floor. As he tried to complete a sit-up on his own, the effort he was putting in was clear. The muscles in his neck were knotted and his face was twisted into a grimace of pain. His hands clasped behind his head and slowly, very slowly, he managed to pull and strain and heave himself up to a sitting position.

'About bloody time,' said Briggs, then he blew his whistle and shouted, 'All change.'

Normally Briggs would hammer one student and then move on to another, but on that day he seemed to have a real bee in his bonnet about Gareth and was sticking to him like glue. He followed him to the squats zone.

There were three other boys there. They started working immediately, but Gareth stood still and wiped the sweat from his brow.

'Get moving,' yelled Briggs.

Gareth lifted his hands up, placed them behind his head, locked his fingers together and started to bend.

'Right down,' said Briggs and put a hand on Gareth's shoulder, pushing him towards the floor.

Gareth went down just a tiny bit further and started to

push himself up, his enormous, lumpy legs straining against his own weight.

Briggs, shouting so we could all hear, yelled at him, 'If you took the time to do a bit more exercise you might shed a few pounds. You need to lose some weight, boy.'

Gareth came to a stop.

'What are you doing?'

He only managed a single word. 'Tired.'

'Tired?' roared Briggs. 'Tired? You've another forty-five seconds. Let's see some movement. Come *on*!'

And that's when things became too much for Gareth. He bent over, placed his hands on his knees and started making this terrible, rasping, choking sound like he couldn't get his breath. And because everyone else had come to a standstill, the sound seemed to get louder with every rasp.

Briggs whacked Gareth hard on the back and shouted, 'Stand up straight!'

But Gareth didn't react. He'd gone purple and then his breathing just stopped. He looked up, staring straight ahead with wide, bulging eyes, and his face went from purple to blue. His eyes rolled up and he slumped to the floor. And with no one talking, no one working, there was nothing to disguise the sound of Gareth's bare skin slap against the floor.

I have never, ever, seen a teacher look as frightened as Briggs did right there.

We were all rushed out of the gym. We could hear the ambulance siren before we'd even got dressed.

Two main things resulted from that event – Briggs never taught circuit training again, and Gareth never took part in another PE lesson.

•

Yet here he was, only eight months on, and I'd just made him run nearly two miles.

I stepped towards him. 'Gareth? Gareth, are you OK?'

He held up a hand, telling me to wait, and nodded.

I placed a hand on his back and said, 'Take it easy, big man. Don't go dying on me.'

Gareth waved me off and managed to say, 'I'm out of breath, that's all.' He looked up, his eyes following the train tracks, looking up towards Penshaw and the steep hill we still had to climb to reach home.

'Sorry, Kyle,' he gasped. 'I just need a few minutes. Go on, you keep going.'

'No way.'

'I mean it,' he said. 'Alex will only give me a bit of a slap, but if he catches you he'll put you in hospital.'

It wasn't even worth considering. I knew for a fact that Alex wouldn't take pity on Gareth, no matter how out of breath he was.

'Look,' I said. 'We got a good start. If we get to the houses we can lose him.'

Gareth shook his head. 'I don't think I can make it. It's got to be another mile, at least, and all uphill.'

We were wasting time. Alex could be on us at any moment. In frustration I looked over the edge of the viaduct. Down below was the river, but running alongside it, at the far side, was a narrow, meandering footpath. It was almost hidden from the world by the trees and bushes on either side. Perfect for Sunday walks and bike rides . . . and pretty good for escape.

'We'll climb down,' I said.

'You're joking!'

'If we keep to the tracks, Alex will find us. If we try to go up towards Penshaw, he'll see us. But if we climb down, we'll have a chance. We can walk to the main road and catch a bus the rest of the way home.'

'But that's still too far to run.'

'We won't need to. Alex won't know we're down there. We can take all the time we like. Come *on*. We can't stand here all day.'

So we kept clear of the tracks – just in case – and made it to the far side of the viaduct. We clambered over the wall and started our descent.

But the slope wasn't just steep, it was a minefield of twisted roots, bushes and brambles. I lost my footing, went head over heels and very nearly smacked my face straight into a tree trunk.

'This is insane,' I cried.

'It was your idea.' Gareth was making his way by shuffling on his hands, heels and backside. 'It would be less painful to get beaten up.'

We reached the path directly below the enormous stone arches of the viaduct.

'You think he'll be there yet?' asked Gareth.

'Who cares? Come on.'

We brushed ourselves down and started walking towards the village. There was a bridge there, a main road and, best of all, a bus stop.

We didn't get very far before we heard the unmistakable voice of Alex cry out from up above. 'You're a dead man, Kyle!'

He was up on the viaduct, leaning over the side.

'You too, Gareth. You better start running.'

'Come on,' I said. 'Keep going.' I pulled him along and we started to run, but it wasn't long before Gareth was out of breath once more and we were still a long, long way from the main road. To our right, the river was deep and wide. To the left, nettles and bushes and weeds, then a vertical cliff face.

'We'll have to find somewhere to hide.'

I looked at the mass of nettles. 'You're going to walk through that?'

But Gareth already was, picking his way towards the bushes. 'You got a better idea?'

I did. I noticed a battered old shopping trolley lying on its side. I could use that as a springboard. So I climbed on top, got my balance and went for it.

I landed badly, tripped, and in an attempt to stay on my feet, I shot forward, straight towards the side of the cliff.

That was when I found something amazing.

ALEX

I have never been so hell bent on getting someone as I was that day. It wasn't what he'd said that did the damage. It was the fact it was Kyle who'd said it.

It was a long time since I'd taken that drawing from the art room and I still thought it looked amazing. I liked to keep an eye on Kyle during art. I made sure I kept my distance. I didn't want anyone to think I was looking up to him or anything, so I always stayed at the other side of the room, but I'd find reasons to walk past his table, not only to see what he was doing, but *how* he was doing it.

I wasn't bad at art myself. There were a few other people in our class that were OK too, but Kyle was something else. When he picked up pastels or paints, he didn't seem to think about it – he just did it. And he worked differently too. Other kids would work in set stages – background, middleground, foreground, just like we were taught. But not Kyle. Kyle would work on small areas – just one at a time – adding block colour, then highlights and detail until that tiny area was perfect. Only then would he move onto the next piece, and he'd work on that until it was complete, and so on. Then, like magic, the jigsaw pieces would all come together to form a whole, seamless image.

I was never jealous. Don't go thinking I was, because I wasn't. While other kids said they wished they could draw like Kyle, I was happy just to watch. There was something about seeing him at work that was enough. It was like watching a top fighter – seeing them weave and dodge without breaking a sweat, then strike back with precision. I'm talking about skill, and that's what Kyle had, an immense amount of skill. He was exceptional, and that's something you don't see very often. He might have been a nerd at times, especially the way he carried on with Gareth and Jamie Spencer, but I had a strange kind of respect for him.

And I reckon that's it. That's the bottom line, because I didn't feel that way about anyone else in the whole school. Not a kid, not a teacher. No one.

So when he said what he did, I just flipped. I felt betrayed. I wanted to kill him.

•

I saw the two of them legging it over the fields. That just made me worse. All I planned on doing – I mean, all I *really* planned on doing – was giving him a hard time, a few slaps, knock him down and that. But now I'd have to chase after them, run cross country just to catch up. Normally I'd have let it go, waiting until the next day, but like I say, I was pretty fired up to begin with, so when I caught them running across the fields, I just saw red. Next thing I knew, I was running after them.

I didn't sprint. Instead, I decided to take it easy. Just a comfortable jog. Kyle had Gareth with him, so even with their head start it wasn't going to take long to catch up with them.

But when I reached the viaduct, I knew something was wrong. The only sure route for Kyle and Gareth to get home was across that viaduct and then up through the fields. I'd be able to see them as clear as day. There was no way, no way on earth they could be up there already. But there was no sign of either of them, which meant only one thing. Somewhere along the route, they'd managed to give me the slip.

I felt like kicking myself. If I'd pushed myself just a little, if I'd kept to a run instead of a jog . . .

I was hit by a whole new wave of anger and slammed my hands on the railings, glaring out over river. I looked down at the trees and bushes and something caught my eye. I could hardly believe it. There they were, tumbling down the slope on the far side of the river. The cheeky bastards *were* trying to give me the slip. If I'd not seen them for myself, I'd never have imagined either would have the balls to climb down there.

My anger reached boiling point. I ran to the other side of the viaduct, leaned over those railings and screamed down at the two of them. Oh, I could have sneaked down there, I could have crept up on them, but I was in a rage, and I wanted them to *know* I was coming.

Kyle's face was a picture.

Gareth looked like he'd filled his pants.

I ran to the point where the bridge met the slope, jumped over the wall and almost threw myself down through those trees. There was no way they were going to get away now.

KYLE

The rock face at the bottom of the cliffs was almost completely covered with ivy and all kinds of climbing weeds. And not just from the ground, but from outcrops further up on the rock face, spilling over the rock in thick leafy curtains. When I stumbled forward, heading straight for that wall of ivy, I thought the cliff behind would break my fall. Instead, my hands went straight through and I very nearly followed.

From nearby, Gareth hissed, 'Get down.'

I was too shocked to speak. I pushed my hands through again, feeling nothing but cold air behind.

The ivy was all twisted and meshed together, but gently, I began pulling it apart like a pair of leafy curtains.

All I could see beyond was pure black nothing.

Gareth snapped me from my trance. 'Get down, Kyle. Quick.'

I gave him a glance, then stared back into the blackness.

'Don't need to,' I said. 'Come here.'

'What?'

'Just come here, will you?' I pointed at the cliff. 'Solid rock, right? Well watch this.'

I stepped forward, moved the ivy aside and disappeared into the darkness. I let the ivy close behind me, turned and looked through the gaps. I could still see Gareth – only just – and I could see the expression of astonishment on his face.

'Can you see me?'

Gareth shook his head. 'Not a thing.'

I pushed my hand through the ivy. 'How about now?'

'I can see your hand. But that's all I can see.'

I parted the ivy and grinned out at him. 'Best come in then. Careful though. Don't pull the leaves.'

As soon as Gareth was in I let the natural curtain close, quickly ruffling the leaves to even it out and make sure there were no obvious gaps.

Gareth started to say, 'I can't believe . . .' but I shushed him to be quiet. Alex would be passing any second now.

We didn't have to wait very long.

'I know you're around here somewhere,' he called. 'You can't hide forever.'

He sounded madder than ever. I could make him out through the tiny gaps in the ivy. He was looking this way and that, towards the river, at the bushes on both sides of the path.

He called out, 'I'll find you.'

Eventually, he looked in our direction, and I could have sworn he was looking at me, and I mean, *right* at me, but a second later he turned his attention back towards the viaduct, cursed and walked out of view.

We stood in the dark, in silence, for ten long seconds.

'Where's he gone?' asked Gareth.

'He must think we doubled back, or climbed up the other side. So long as he's gone, I really don't care.'

Gareth turned round to take a better look at the inside of the cave.

'Jesus,' he said. 'It's huge.'

'Well I wouldn't say huge,' I said, 'but certainly big enough to hide in.'

'Hang on.' He began searching his pockets – he kept all kinds of junk in there, and after a moment's hunt, he pulled out a small, thin penlight and turned it on.

'How far did you look?' he said.

For some reason I'd assumed the cave was only a metre or so deep. Now that we had some illumination I could see that I was wrong.

'My god. I didn't realise it was *that* big'

'You could hide a car in here,' said Gareth, walking further into the cave.

I held out my arms like it was all mine and said, 'Hell of a find, eh?'

Gareth nodded. 'Hell of a find.'

As our eyes were adjusting to the darkness, and with a little help from Gareth's penlight, we could see just how big the cave was. It must have been four metres deep, and at least three metres wide. And it was cold. Even though it was a hot summer day outside, there was an unmistakable chill inside the cave.

I rubbed my hands over the wall. Grime and soil clung to the rock, but it was dry. There was a slight echo in there and for some reason our footsteps seemed to sound a little louder than they should. It all gave the cave an uneasy, spooky feel, and apart from a few rocks and boulders, it was also completely empty. No litter. Not a single bit. In a place like this, I would have expected to find all kinds of rubbish, probably a few empty lager cans or something, but there was nothing. Nothing at all.

In little more than a whisper, I said, 'I think we're the first people to find this. Hey, there aren't any cave paintings, are there? This place could be worth a fortune if there are.'

'Not by the look of it,' said Gareth. He ran his penlight over the walls. 'Just a big empty hole in the rock.'

I was grinning again – a great big, fat, shit-eating grin. 'Yeah, but what a place, eh? This could be perfect.'

'For what?'

'A camp. A clubhouse. A hideout, man. A totally secret hideout. What do you think?'

Gareth weighed up the idea and began to nod. 'Yeah. Yeah, I suppose so. You couldn't get much more secret than this. The perfect place for a hideout.' He held out a trembling hand towards me. 'The perfect place for a *murder*. Bwahahahaha.'

I stepped back. 'Get off.'

He came towards me, arms outstretched. 'Bwahahahaha.'

I slapped his hand away. 'That's not funny.' But at the same time, I looked about the cave and it got me thinking. 'This place would look good with a few candles though. Totally Gothic. We could bring sandwiches and crisps and things – comics, a few mags.'

'Porn mags?'

'Why not? No one will find them.'

Gareth's eyes widened. 'Got it! Ghost stories. Can't get more Gothic than that. We could read them out and stuff.' Gareth wasn't just a dab hand with his urban legends, he was horror mad. He had stacks of books; his bedroom walls were covered with posters of Freddie Kruger, Chucky, Frankenstein and other monsters and ghouls.

'Read them?' I said. 'I don't think I'll be any good.'

'What are you talking about? When we did *Macbeth*, you were great – you really hammed it up.'

'I was rubbish. Besides, I stutter when I read.'

'Well something else then. How about a séance?'

'You want to do a séance? You want to sit in a dark cave, with candles burning and talk to dead people?'

'Hell yeah! This place is probably crawling with spirits. We could go one further, light *black* candles and say the Devil's Prayer,' he ended with a dark, guttural chuckle.

I just stared at him. 'The what?'

'It something my granda told me. When I was a bairn, he used to wave his finger and say, "Not for a bet, not for a dare. Never say the Devil's Prayer", and my gran would go nuts, telling him not to say such stupid things.'

'Why? What is it?'

'The Lord's Prayer – backwards. They reckon if you say it while looking into the flame of a black candle, and you say it right, you see the face of the Devil. It can scare you to death. Literally.'

'For real?'

Gareth shrugged. 'Dunno. I've never met anyone daft enough to see it through.'

It seemed ridiculous. 'Why would they? I mean, you're not

going to actually see the Devil, are you? Not really. So you're not really going to die.'

'Would *you* do it?'

I laughed at the idea, but he pushed his question.

'Seriously,' he said. 'Would you?'

The more I thought about it, the less funny it seemed.

'Well it's stupid, isn't it?'

'But would you say it? If we got the candles, would you actually do it?'

'No way.'

Gareth pointed a chubby finger. 'That's the point. It's a rite of passage, isn't it? It's not about what you think will happen, it's about what *might* happen – that million to one chance that you'll die or go mad. It's a test of courage. All societies have something or other – something really dangerous to prove you're a man.'

'Oh right, like walking on hot coals. I've heard of that.'

'Yeah. But it could be anything, so long as it scares the shit out of you – parachuting, bungee jumping . . .'

'Humiliating Alex Crow in front of the whole class?'

Gareth considered. 'I'd take the hot coals over that, saying the Devil's Prayer as I walked across.'

I cracked up then. Gareth laughed too, but a voice from outside cut us short.

'I know you're still here.'

It was Alex.

'Jesus,' I whispered.

'You think he heard us?'

'Keep quiet. And turn the torch off. He'll never see us.'

Gareth clicked off his penlight and we were plunged into

darkness. The only light was the pinpoints of sunlight cutting through the wall of ivy.

Another call from outside; this time closer. 'I'll find you. And when I do . . .'

Gareth whispered, 'If he comes in here, we're dead.'

He was right. And with the ivy hiding us from the world outside, Alex could even take his time. If no one could see him, no one could stop him.

ALEX

By the time I reached the path there was mud streaked on my trousers, I was covered in scratches and severely pissed off. I didn't dwell on it though, I ran along the path, jumping across where it dipped and sloped, glancing left and right just in case the two of them were hiding. I only had to go so far to realise that's exactly what they must have done. There was no way Gareth could have run this far. I doubled back and started searching.

There were loads of bushes down there. Lots of dark places to hide – under trees, among the bushes, or places where they clung to the base of those cliffs. Kyle could be anywhere. He'd only have to lie flat and he'd be invisible. But it wouldn't be so easy for Gareth. He wasn't just fat. He was too or three sizes *beyond* fat. It didn't matter where he tried to hide, I was sure I'd find him sooner or later – a flash of ginger hair, a load of flattened bushes, the crack of a branch as he tried to roll further into his hidey hole.

But there was nothing!

The more I looked, the more frustrated I became. I started shouting at them, about what I was going to do. 'If I don't get you now, Kyle, it will be ten times worse tomorrow.'

Like Kyle was stupid enough to stand up and say, 'Well in that case, look – we're over here. Come and get the two of us.'

But I said it anyway, just for sheer hell of it.

I stood looking up at the ivy crawling over the rock face. For a second I wondered if they could have climbed up there, if they could be hiding at the top. I came so close to grabbing that ivy and going after them. But I was pulling at straws. Gareth couldn't have climbed up there, not even with a ladder.

I spat on the grass, turned and decided to head for home.

•

My dad didn't have a history of belting my mam. That only happened once, back when I was ten years old, before I started at the club.

It was a Tuesday evening, a regular pub night for my dad. He'd bought our car from some bloke and was paying for it weekly. At least that's what he told us. Either way, there was always twenty quid put aside behind an old carriage clock on the mantelpiece, and it was never touched. This particular Tuesday he got himself ready, checked himself in the mirror with the same miserable grunt and went to get the money.

A second later, he shouted, 'Meg?'

I looked up. 'What's the matter?'

He didn't answer, but shouted at the door, louder, 'Meg!'

My mam walked in, drying her hands on a tea towel. 'You still here?'

'Where's the money?'

'What money?'

'The money for the car.'

'Behind the clock, where it always is.'

'You think I'd ask if it was there?'

'Have you looked properly?'

He grabbed the clock, lifted it up and slammed it back down. 'It's not *there*.'

'Well I haven't touched it.'

'You have before.'

'Once. To buy food, and I made sure you knew.' She looked at me. 'You haven't seen it have you, pet?'

I tried to sound casual. 'No, Mam.' It worked on her, but my dad's eyes were filled with suspicion.

'You telling the truth, boy?'

I could feel my face going red, but I stood my ground. 'Honest.'

'Well it was there on Thursday,' said my mam. 'I always put it there every Thursday.' Then she looked at my dad. 'You wanted money Saturday. Said you were short, wanted to put something on a horse. You didn't pick it up by mistake, did you?'

'What? You saying I've stolen my own money?'

'You've got money in your wallet.'

He jabbed a finger at the clock. '*That's* the money for the car. It's no one's business what's in my fucking wallet.'

'Will! Not in front of Alex.' She shook her head. 'Well, you'll just not have to have a drink tonight.'

And that was it. He lashed out a hand right across her face, knocked her back two steps. 'Don't you *ever* tell me what to do.'

I expected her to scream or cry or run upstairs, but she just stood there, a hand on her face, eyes wide like she couldn't believe what he'd done.

'Go and find me twenty quid,' he shouted. 'Now!'

A tear rolled down her right cheek, but she didn't move. She moved her hand from her face and saw the blood from her split lip. When she spoke, her voice was low and controlled: 'Get out.'

'You what?'

'You heard me.'

'Yes, I did, I can hardly believe my fucking ears. Now get that money before you get another.'

She stared at him for three, maybe four seconds, then said, 'Fine.' She picked up the phone and began jabbing at buttons.

My dad leaned against the mantelpiece, all cock-sure and confident. 'Who you calling, Meg? The police? You think they care what happens behind closed doors?'

'I'm not calling the police.' She let the blood on her lip run unattended. 'I'm calling Joe.'

My dad almost laughed. 'Joe?'

'That's right. And when he hears what you've done he'll be straight round with about five of his friends – you know his friends, don't you?'

This was just before I'd started training with Carlos, when my dad was getting on quite well with Joe, but he knew fine well that he wouldn't take kindly to his younger sister getting a smack across the face. He was like that, Joe, big and tough up front – a real gangster – but he also had a saying: 'I can't abide people fighting below their belt', which was a way of saying he didn't like big guys picking on little guys, and he made it quite clear that this included men hitting women.

My mam waited for the call to be picked up.

'Pat, hi. It's Meg.'

She didn't get any further. My dad snatched the phone off her and covered the mouthpiece.

'You say one word and I'll . . .'

'You'll what? Hit me again? Kill me? It'll be nothing compared to what Joe will do to you.'

I think they'd forgotten I was still in the room. My dad suddenly seemed nervous. His eyes flicked about before settling back on my mam. 'Just . . . don't say anything, OK? We get on well with Joe and Pat. Let's keep this between us, eh?'

My mam sat up slightly. 'Say you're sorry.'

'What?'

'If you say you're sorry, then I'll consider it.'

'Jesus, Meg. You've lost twenty quid. You accused me of stealing it, what do expect me to do?'

'I don't expect you to lash out. Now say you're sorry or hand me the phone. Pat's still there. She'll know that something is going on.'

Again, his eyes flicked about, as if looking to find the answer somewhere in the front room.

'All right,' he said at last. 'I'm sorry. I'm sorry I hit you. But . . .'

She held up her hand to stop him. 'That's enough. Don't go spoiling it by throwing blame.'

'I said it, didn't I?'

'Now hand me the phone.'

With a fair level of uncertainty, my dad handed over the handset. My mam kept her eyes fixed on him and took it. 'Thank you.' Then she lifted it to her ear. 'Pat, hello again. Sorry about that. No, nothing wrong – just having a heated debate with Will. You know what he's like.' And with the blood drying on her chin she maintained a pleasant voice and held a perfectly ordinary conversation.

My dad never lifted a hand to her again.

•

But for some reason, after he killed Jim Banks, everything changed. Arguments started out of nothing and they became more and more common. But worse than that, they became more aggressive. My dad was always on edge, forever ready to snap. And he did snap, with increasing frequency. I didn't see a lot, but I'd often hear things. Shouting, getting louder and louder and then a crack. My mam crying. Gentle voices. My dad saying he was sorry, but she'd made him do it.

At first, the only marks were the kind that faded fast. Nothing to worry the neighbours about. Nothing to phone Joe about.

But maybe Joe was no longer a threat to my dad. Maybe that's why he didn't hold back so much. Joe was implicated in the murder of Jim Banks. He might not know who'd killed him, but it was Joe who came up with the plan to move the body and cover up the murder. With that hanging over him, he wasn't very likely to send his heavies round to belt my dad. Now I'm not saying my dad knew this, or had given it any thought, or had even mentioned it to my mam, but for some reason the balance had shifted in our house and the threat of a phone call to Joe didn't seem to matter anymore. My dad's violence towards my mum was increasing, and the marks were beginning to show.

•

On the night I got home after chasing Kyle and Gareth, my mam was sitting on the sofa, watching television; my dad was in the chair, filling out a crossword in the newspaper.

'All right?' I muttered — our usual greeting.

My dad ignored me, but my mam looked up with a smile and said, 'About time, Alex. I didn't think you had detention tonight.'

'He gets detention every night,' said my dad, his eyes never leaving his newspaper.

'Not tonight,' I said. 'I just had some stuff to do.'

'Give me five minutes, pet,' said my mam. 'I'll get your tea on.'

That's when I noticed her right eye. It was swollen, making it appear half closed. There was a tiny cut too, which had been cleaned, but the skin was red. There was no doubt in my mind what this was — after all, I've seen my fair share of fights — but I asked her all the same.

'What happened to your face?'

My dad's paper rustled as he refolded it.

'Oh this,' she said, a nervous smile on dry lips, two fingers touching the skin just below the mark. 'I think I must have been daydreaming. I turned too fast and walked straight into the kitchen door.'

As an excuse, it was straight out of a TV soap, and as obvious as the swelling around her eye.

I just smiled back. 'You want to watch that door. If it thinks it can get away with it once, it might try every time you pass.'

The comment was aimed firmly at my dad. He knew it too, and finally looked up, but he said nothing.

On any other day, I might have left it there, but I was still wound up over Kyle and Gareth. Seeing the state of my mam's eye just pushed me over the edge. I felt no fear in pressing the point. 'If that door tries anything else, you want to get straight on the phone. The police don't tolerate violent furniture.'

My mam laughed and shook her head. Her empty wine glass explained her good humour, but my dad was stone cold sober and said what he'd said two years back. 'Police don't care what goes on behind closed doors.'

I couldn't hold back, and quite calmly, I replied, 'It all depends which doors you're talking about. All kinds of things go on behind closed doors. Even toilet doors.'

He placed his pen flat against the newspaper and glared at me. Either my mam felt the atmosphere or she just had good timing.

'Right,' she said, 'I'll get the oven on, see what I can find in the freezer for you.'

As she got up I held my dad's gaze – something that would normally warrant a crack on the head, but tonight things were different. The state of my mam's face, together with her drunken complacency had tipped the balance and I saw him for what he was – a bully with an easy target. He suddenly seemed very small in that chair, and for the first time in my life I wasn't afraid of him.

He sat forward. 'Are you threatening me, boy?'

I simply nodded and replied, 'That's right,' and waited for what he'd come back with.

He continued to stare. There was a flicker of a grin – a twitch, no more – and with the slightest shake to his voice, he said, 'Watch your step, boy.'

KYLE

I arrived home to the smell of pizza coming from the kitchen and music coming from upstairs. The oven was low, and according to the kitchen clock I was well over an hour late.

I dropped my bag and ventured upstairs to see what was going on. The music sounded like it was coming from the nursery, from Christopher's room, but that didn't make any sense.

I walked towards the open door to find the room a total mess. The carpet, the one that I had chosen, the one with the planes and trains and teddy bears on it, had been rolled back and pushed to one side. The cot that I'd helped put together was dismantled and leaning against the wall, and my mum was standing in front of that wonderfully bright tall-boy wardrobe, with a paintbrush in one hand and a tin of cream paint in the other.

'What's going on?' I asked.

'I'm decorating.'

'I can see that.'

She smiled, put down the tin and came over. She kissed me on the forehead and said, 'Then it's a stupid question, isn't it?'

'Yeah, but . . .'

I stopped. What could I say? I suddenly felt uncomfortable. I felt queasy. I mean, I knew it had to be done at some point, but that didn't make it any easier.

The lampshade was gone. I looked again at the cot, wondering where she'd put the mobile.

'You've been busy,' I said, trying to swallow the lump in my throat.

'Yes. I did the walls first.'

My god! The walls. I hadn't even noticed that she'd painted over the little white rabbits. It wasn't immediately obvious because she'd used a similar shade of blue to the wallpaper that she'd painted over, obliterating each and every rabbit.

She gave me a reassuring smile and placed a hand on my shoulder. 'We have to move on at some point. And if we want an office or a study, then it's going to look pretty silly with bunny wallpaper. Imagine studying for exams with a room full of rabbits. Anyway, how come you're so late?'

'Oh, erm, we got talking and missed the bus, so we decided to walk to the next stop, and then the next. By that time we were halfway home so we kept the money and walked the rest of the way.'

'You must have walked very slowly.'

I shrugged. 'You know Gareth.'

She gave me one of her serious 'mother' frowns and said,

'That's not very nice.'

'I'm just saying he drags his feet. That's all.'

After tea I went up to my room. I looked at the mess that covered my desk. Pens, pencils, pastels and paints. An unfinished painting, a sketch of a dragon that had gone wrong and my growing pile of fantasy art books.

I sat down through habit rather than interest and half-heartedly began sketching. I drew a general outline of the cave, scrapped it and started again with a map of where it was in relation to the river, the viaduct and the little road bridge at the village.

The doorbell went and my mum shouted up, 'Kyle. It's Gareth.'

I crumpled the map and chucked it in the bin.

I didn't have to get up. Gareth spent more time here than in his own house and almost immediately I heard him pounding up the stairs.

As he entered the room he held up a pile of books. 'Research,' he announced. 'Some of the scariest stories on the planet. The crème de la crème of gruesome tales and ghostly horror.'

I looked at the books. 'Eh?'

'For the cave, stupid. Ghost stories, horror stories, all kinds.'

'Ah, right. Nice one.' I took one off him and started to flick through.

'It stinks of paint out there. You decorating?'

'Mum is. Christopher's room.'

'Oh.'

Silence.

'You OK?'

137

I kept my eyes on the book. 'It's got to be done sometime.'

Gareth went to his regular place in the room and tapped on the side of the small glass vivarium that stood on my bookshelves.

'Evening, Harold,' he said.

'It can't hear you.'

'You say that every time I talk to him.'

'And you talk to it every time I tell you it can't hear.'

'You don't know that, though, do you?'

I looked across, at the vivarium where 'Harold' – as Gareth had named it – was sitting perfectly still. 'If it can hear, then it's hardly likely to understand English. Your voice will just sound like a meaningless rumble.'

'I wish I had a pet scorpion.'

'Feel free. Take it with you.'

'No chance. Can you imagine what my mum would say if she saw him?'

I slapped the book closed and said, 'Gareth. It's not a "he". It's an "it". A "thing". It can't hear you and it won't run after a ball. As pets go, it's about as exciting as a dead tortoise and as interesting as a brick.'

'I don't get you. He's so cool. I mean, a real, live genuine scorpion. It's big and black and terrifying. One sting from one of these can kill you.'

'If it could kill you, you wouldn't be able to buy them in the pet shop.'

'Yeah, I know. But in the movies . . .'

'I read the book. It says it's no worse than a bee sting. They use emperor scorpions in the movies because they *look* scary. In reality, the ones that really can kill you are little pale things, about the size of a thumbnail – they look about as scary as a worm.'

'So why didn't you buy one of them instead?'

'Because they can kill you, dip-shit.'

I glanced across at the scorpion. Usually it just sat there. Sometimes it shifted dirt about the floor of its home or tried to bury itself. It was about four inches long, shiny and black. It did, indeed, look the part of a deadly killer, but once you'd got used to the fact that you weren't going to get much action out of it, the novelty of owning a dangerous pet grew thin very quickly.

Gareth glanced around the room, at the pictures on the walls. 'You never draw him.'

'What?'

'You draw just about everything else, but never the scorpion.'

'Cut the psychology, will you? Besides, I concentrate on fantasy art now.'

'I bet you do,' said Gareth, making a wanking motion with his right hand – smack-smack-smack.

'Ha ha. Very funny.'

Still chuckling, Gareth turned back to the vivarium and tapped on the glass.

'Have you picked him up yet?'

'Not a chance. It's too aggressive. The book says they're supposed to be quite docile, but not Harold.'

Gareth whirled around. 'Hey, you said it.'

'Said what?'

'"Harold",' he announced with a grin. 'You called him "Harold".'

'A slip of the tongue, Gareth. It doesn't mean I suddenly like the thing.'

'This is insane. You don't think . . . I mean, you don't actually believe your mum meant it as . . .' he quietened his voice to a whisper, 'a replacement.'

'Well, no, I don't think she meant it like that, but I think her counsellor probably did. It just didn't feel like something my mum would say, you know? She's never been one for pets before, and then one day we're in the town and suddenly she starts heading over to the pet shop, saying, "Every boy should have a pet. Let's go and see what they have, eh?"'

Gareth seemed to be weighing this up, but he didn't reply. He dropped his eyes and I felt the need to justify what I'd said.

'It just felt too convenient,' I said. 'One minute I've got a brother, the next I don't. Then it's like, hey, never mind, have this instead.'

'Maybe they thought it would help, that you were upset about things.'

I snapped. 'Too bloody right I was upset. But I certainly didn't want a cat or a dog as some kind of second prize.'

'So you went for something a little less fluffy?'

Gareth spelling it out like that made me feel a bit stupid. 'I suppose so.'

'A scorpion?'

'Actually, I chose a tarantula, but they were too expensive. The scorpions were in the next tank along.'

Gareth turned back to look at the creature. 'I still think it's a cool pet.'

'A psychopathic scorpion?'

Gareth laughed. 'Called Harold.'

I couldn't help giving in to a small grin. 'Should have called him Alex Crow.'

•

The next morning, I met Gareth in his usual spot and we headed towards the bus stop. His very first words were, 'Have you read any of those stories, for the cave?'

There weren't many other kids that used our bus stop, but I still had to say, 'Keep your voice down, eh.'

He looked about and asked, 'But did you?'

'Not really,' I admitted. 'I tried a few, but I had other things on my mind.'

Gareth nodded like he knew, then asked, 'Like what?'

'Just stuff.' Mostly it was stuff I really didn't want to talk about, so before he could quiz me I got in quick with, 'Like the fact that Alex is probably going to be on this bus.'

'He'll be upstairs,' said Gareth. 'He always is.'

I gave him a firm stare, knowing I shouldn't really need to spell it out.

Finally, his eyes widened and he took a sharp breath. 'Well maybe he's forgotten. Maybe . . .'

Too late. The bus was turning the corner.

It pulled up, the doors opened and we stepped on.

I took a quick look around.

Gareth was right behind me. 'Maybe he *did* forget.'

'Fine by me.' I quickly walked to my regular seat and sat down.

Gareth pushed in next to me. 'It doesn't matter, you know. It's more fun if we make them up.'

'What?'

'The stories. The ghost stories. We can just make them up.'

'Yeah. All right.'

I looked out through the window and drifted off.

Gareth nudged me. 'Are you OK?'

I sighed. 'I've just got a few things on my mind.'

Gareth sat for a while. Eventually, he said, 'Christopher's room?'

I gave him a sarcastic look. 'Well give that boy a prize!'

'Right. Right.'

He finally got the hint and left me alone for the rest of the journey, but as we stepped off the bus and walked towards the school gates he started again. 'It's such a cool hideout, isn't it?'

I sighed, but nodded.

'The cave, I mean.'

'I know.'

'We've got to keep it a secret, haven't we? We can't let anyone know about that cave, and I mean *anyone*. Not even Jamie.'

'Yeah, I know.'

'Otherwise we'll go down there one night and find half the school there.'

'I know, Gareth. I get the point.'

'So just us, yeah?'

'Yes.'

We walked a little further. I could almost feel Gareth grinning next to me, dying to say something more about the cave. It didn't take long. As we stepped through the school gates he couldn't hold back any more.

'It's going to be so cool. You know, once we've got it

decked out and looking like a real camp. No one has ever had a hideout like this.'

From behind us, came the unmistakable voice of Alex Crow. 'But there's no hideout now, is there?'

I couldn't believe I hadn't looked back. I couldn't believe he'd slipped my mind. I was hardly able to get my words out. 'A- Alex.'

'Remember what I said about it being ten times worse if you didn't show yourself? Well guess what, Kyle? I lied. It's going to be a lot more.'

Kids around us had stopped walking. They had sensed that something was up and didn't want to miss the possibility of a fight.

The only way I could see of getting out of this was through sense, reason, and possibly pleading.

'Look,' I said. 'This is stupid.'

'Funny, I don't see it that way. I don't like being made a fool of, and I don't like people laughing at me. So I'll give you a choice, you can stand like a man and get what's coming, or you can run.'

I'd been told many, many times that there is only one sure way to deal with someone like Alex Crow. Bullies operate through fear and intimidation. It doesn't matter how big they are, if you stand firm and show no fear they will be forced to back off.

And that's what I did. I stood as tall as I could and I told him clearly, with about fifteen or twenty other kids present, 'I'm not scared of you, Alex. And I'm not going to run.'

'Good,' he said, and punched me so hard I nearly left the ground.

I found myself sitting on my arse with pain exploding across my jaw and a deafening sound in both ears. It felt like I'd been hit with a sledgehammer.

'Get up,' he ordered.

The crowd around us seemed to tighten, sealing up any chance of escape. Someone shouted, 'Go on, deck him,' and another replied, 'He already did, stupid.'

Alex repeated, 'Get up.'

'I think I'm fine here.'

In a moment of insane bravery, Gareth grabbed Alex's sleeve and said, 'Come on, man. Leave him alone.'

Alex swung out and hit him across the face with the back of his hand. Gareth staggered against the crowd.

Alex glared down at me, and I was sure he was going to drag me up or belt me while I sat there, but before he got the chance a voice rang out, 'Move aside, out of my way. Move, now!'

It was Mr Slate. He must have been crossing the road right when Alex punched me.

The crowd were pushed aside as Slate made his way towards us. He actually shoved Alex out of the way in order to get at me.

As he grabbed me by the collar and yanked me to my feet, Alex tried to melt into the crowd.

'Get back here, Crow. Don't you dare move.'

The crowd started to disperse but Slate shouted out, 'You can all stay right where you are. I want every one of you to hear this.'

He kept a tight hold of my collar and with his other hand he grabbed Alex and pulled us together.

'No one, and I mean *no one*, fights on school premises. Do you understand?'

I tried to defend myself, saying, 'I was just . . .'

'Be quiet, boy! Two hundred lines. For each of you.'

Alex snorted. A punishment like that was about as much of a threat to him as I was.

Slate released us from his grip and folded his arms. 'I haven't finished. You, Crow, you're no stranger to detention, are you?'

Alex didn't answer.

'Well, you'll be pleased to know that tonight it's *my* detention.'

I was shocked. 'Tonight? It's Friday. I thought we have to have twenty-four hours notice.'

'I'm giving you more than enough notice. I'll even phone your parents personally, just to make sure they know you'll be late.'

Alex wasn't phased. 'Big deal.'

'Oh, it will be. Believe me. I'll be sure to add that you will most likely be *very* late, because neither of you will leave until you have completed every single line. I'll see you both at three thirty.'

I couldn't believe this was happening. I mean, detention? For getting beaten up? It was totally unfair.

I tried again. 'But, sir –'

Slate shut me up with a single bony finger pointed right at my face. 'If I hear one more word from you, I will double your punishment. Understand?'

I kept my lips tight and nodded.

'I will not tolerate fighting. Not by anyone!' Without waiting for a reaction or argument, he marched off towards the school.

The show was over and the other kids began to move away.

'You OK?'

I looked up. It was Gareth. I shrugged, then I carefully touched a finger to my chin and winced. It hurt like hell. At least he hadn't drawn blood. At least I hadn't cried.

'I think I got off light.'

Gareth nodded, but his face showed another concern. 'Do you think he heard what I said?'

'About what?'

'About the hideout, about the . . .' He stopped, as though he'd just made the biggest mistake of his life. I turned to see what he was looking at.

Alex was still standing there, right behind me.

I expected him to sneer and thank us for letting him know, but if he had heard anything, he didn't mention it. He just leaned forward, pushed his face right up to mine and whispered, 'I'll see *you* after detention.'

•

At three thirty, while the rest of the school were leaving for the weekend, I sat in a chair at the front of our maths class. Alex was to my right, sitting two tables away. We each had a pad of lined, A4 paper. We each had a pen. We had not been told to start.

Slate sat at his desk and concentrated on marking books.

He didn't look up.

This went on for a long time.

As the seconds ticked by I found myself restless. All I wanted to do was to get on with the task and get out of there, but Slate paid us no attention.

I glanced over at Alex. He was twiddling his pen over and over in his fingers. He was staring at it, watching his fingers work the pen faster.

Eventually, hoping to spur the teacher on, I let out a small sigh.

Immediately, Slate snapped his head up and glared at me. 'Silence.'

I ended up staring at the clock high up on the wall, watching the second hand click its way around. Four whole minutes passed before Slate pushed back his chair and stood up. He took a marker pen from his drawer and walked over to the white board.

'Now, two hundred lines,' he said and began to write.

I got my pen at the ready, expecting Slate to bang out a few words and move out of the way so we could copy them down.

But he didn't. He kept writing.

All I could do was stare at the board, first in disbelief, and then in horror as he continued to write, and write, and write. It looked as though he was never going to stop. When he finally stepped aside I felt real, physical sickness as I read the line he'd written on that board:

I will not partake in physical or psychological acts of aggressive violence with or towards any other member of this educational establishment.

'You've got to be kidding,' said Alex.

I felt the same way. We were going to be here all night.

'I never kid,' replied Slate.

'How about just having "I will not fight at school"?' said Alex.

I had to agree, and suggested, 'Or "No fighting". What's wrong with that?'

Slate didn't even flicker a smile. 'Don't joke with me, either of you. There is a simple rule when it comes to giving lines – one, single, clear sentence that reflects the incident. I see no problem with this sentence, so if you want to get home at some time this evening, you will begin writing. Now.'

With reluctance, that's what we did.

But I soon decided that I had one slight advantage. I *knew* that I could do the work, whereas Alex – over the past six months – had become a work-shy thug. Even if I went at a steady pace, I was more than confident that I would finish long before him.

The traditional technique in writing lines was to write the first sentence at the top of the page, and then do vertical columns of each word, one at a time. But this technique didn't work when you had a sentence so long that it wouldn't fit on one line. Slate was a bastard. He made two hundred lines feel like four hundred.

I was only getting about seventeen of these ridiculous lines to a page, so after I'd written three full sides I decided I needed a short rest. I put my pen down, stretched my fingers and looked across at Alex.

I fully expected him to be asleep, doodling or sitting back in his chair with a look of defiance on his face.

But he wasn't.

Alex had his head down and he was writing. He was writing line after line after line, and at a ferocious speed. He'd already filled four sides. I did the maths in a second – that was over sixty lines!

Alex caught sight of me watching him and smiled. That smile was packed with menace, and it all became frighteningly clear. If Alex finished first, he'd be let out first. He would stand at the school gates and wait until I was released.

Oh shit.

I was going to die.

I grabbed my pen and joined the race.

I knew I was way behind, and I had to do whatever I could to catch up. I kept my writing small; less movement, more speed. With each line, my writing got smaller and more crammed until eventually I achieved the impossible – I managed to cram that whole, evil sentence onto a single line. Once I'd done that I felt like I was really making progress. But this was no time for patting myself on the back – there wasn't even time to look up and check how Alex was doing. The only way of winning this race was to work and work and work.

I was only aware of Slate looking once. He probably thought we were working like this simply because *he* had set the detention.

The only sound in that room was when one of us took a second or two to shake our aching hands, stretch fingers, or tear off another completed page from our A4 pad.

Pain from my hand spread out over the whole of my forearm. Even my shoulder was beginning to ache, but I kept going, knocking out line after line, right up until I heard the words I had dreaded.

'Finished.' Alex pulled his pages together and stood up. He approached Slate's desk and as he placed his papers down, he turned his head and gave me a quick wink.

I looked down at my own work. I had been putting markers at ten-line intervals to save me having to recount. If my markers were correct, I had at least another twenty lines to go.

Slate snatched the papers up and Alex made for the door.

'Wait,' commanded Slate.

Alex stopped and turned back.

Slate was going through each page with a red pen in his right hand. Every so often he would cross out an entire line. The further into the pages he went, the more lines were crossed out. Eventually he handed the sheets back to Alex.

'Another thirty,' he said.

'What?' Alex looked mortified.

'You've rushed them. Some of these lines are nothing more than meaningless scrawl. Another thirty, and make sure they are legible.'

Alex clenched his fists, crumpling the sheets in his left hand and scowled. I actually thought he was going to attack the teacher.

Slate didn't even flinch, he just stared back. He didn't take his eyes off Alex until he backed down and returned to his desk.

I was back to work before Alex had sat down. A few minutes later I managed to complete my final line. I got up, rushed to the desk and I handed my papers over.

Slate examined them, crossed out eight and asked for another ten to make up for it.

'You only crossed out eight,' I said.

'Would you like me to make it twenty?'

'No, sir.'

'Then shut your mouth and get to work.'

The race continued.

I knew I was ahead, but it wasn't by far. I did my best to keep up the same speed until at last, with immense relief, I stood up and approached the teacher's desk.

Alex stopped working and stared at me. His expression was not pleasant.

I breathed a sigh of relief as Slate nodded and tore up all of my work.

Without looking at me, he simply said, 'Go.'

I headed straight for the exit – a side entrance next to the art block that I use each morning and afternoon. I sprinted the last few metres, grabbed the handles and pulled.

The doors banged against their locks, but remained tight shut.

'Oh no.'

And when I turned around, I froze.

Alex was walking towards me, taking his time and humming a tune. As he got closer, he casually folded his arms.

'This is your first detention, isn't it, Kyle?'

I couldn't answer.

'I guess you didn't know that these doors get locked at four o'clock.'

I just stood and stared. Alex was standing in front of me. I was trapped. The door behind me was locked and Alex was blocking my only escape.

'Well,' he said. 'What are you going to do now?'

'You can't get me in here, Alex.'

'Why not? There's no one about.'

'Slate is still here.'

'He's at the other side of the school, and he'll be marking for hours. He probably didn't expect either of us to finish for another half hour at least.'

'We'll be straight back in detention.'

'No skin off my nose. I get detention every other night.'

He wouldn't kill me. Not on school grounds.

I clenched my knuckles, swallowed and said, 'Right . . . Come on then.'

Alex smiled. 'Are you serious?'

'Yeah. Come on, let's get it over with.'

'Fair enough.'

Alex Crow walked forward with slow, purposeful strides. He clenched a fist and smacked it twice into his open left hand.

With the exception of the beating I'd taken that morning, I'd never had a proper fight in my life. All I could do was to hold my fists up and wonder if I'd get a chance to land a single punch. I expected to be on the floor, bleeding and in pain, at any moment.

But Alex didn't hit me. To my surprise (and relief) he simply held out a hand.

I didn't quite understand.

'Quits,' said Alex.

'Quits?'

'Yeah. Quits. To be honest, I'm not even sure why I was so hung up on getting you.'

'Because I made a joke about you needing more worksheets.'

Alex frowned as he recalled the incident. 'Yeah.'

Oh *shiiiit*. I'd just reminded him!

Stupid, *stupid*, *stupid*.

But he only grinned and said, 'I suppose it *was* pretty funny. Come on. Let's go.'

I didn't move. 'You don't plan on getting me as soon as we're outside?'

'I could beat you up here if I wanted, Kyle. But I don't. So let's go.'

I was nervous. I was convinced something was up, but what choice did I have? None, that was what. So I gave in and with a feeling of dread, I decided to go along with it.

We walked together, with just a short gap between us. The school was quiet and our trainers clapped unusually loud on the floor. We never saw a teacher or a student all the way to the main entrance, which made me realise just how right Alex had been. He really could have beaten me up by those doors and no one would have stopped him.

Even with that in mind, I got a surge of panic as we approached the main doors. Slate might have been busy, but he was still here; he was still in the school. There would be other teachers here too, and the caretaker was bound to be about somewhere. But once I stepped through those doors I would be outside. There would just be me and Alex.

He noticed that I had slowed down and asked, 'What's up?'

'Erm . . .' I couldn't think of a single excuse.

'It's OK, Kyle. I said quits and I meant it.' Then he laughed and added, 'Besides, that was one cool move you made the other day. You totally disappeared. I still don't have a clue how you did it.'

I actually laughed. 'Yeah. I suppose it was pretty cool.'

As we walked through the doors, Alex continued. 'You're like the Invisible Man or something. You should be on stage, doing magic tricks. How the hell do you hide something the size of Gareth?'

He said it with good humour, as though he wasn't expecting an answer, and again I laughed, hardly able to believe that Alex was prepared to joke about the whole thing rather than beat me senseless over it.

ALEX

I'd planned to wait until after detention. Get him one on one, make sure there was no one around to interrupt or interfere, then I'd kick the living shit out of him. Kyle had made me look like an idiot in class and a fool down by the viaduct.

I knew they had some kind of hideout. Course I did. I'm not stupid. So when Gareth slipped up, he only confirmed what I was already thinking. I mean, you can't hide someone like him in a bunch of nettles, can you?

The thing is, over the course of that detention, doing the same line over and over, my mind wandered from Kyle to home, and the reason I was spending more and more time after school sitting in a classroom doing pointless tasks like this. I was sick of it. And not just of detention. I was sick of wandering the streets afterwards, filling out time to avoid going home. I certainly didn't want to hang round shops like the morons in the mall. But a hideout, down by the river.

That could be OK, and the more I thought about it, the more inviting it became.

The problem with the mall wasn't the banality of wandering round shops, it was the wankers I'd end up hanging out with. I'd been there enough times now, seeing the likes of Matlock and Hughes getting their kicks by nicking Pick 'n' Mix or laughing at passers by. I could actually imagine myself going over, having a laugh, doing the same mindless stuff. And that freaked me out. I couldn't bear the thought that I was anything like them, but it made one thing very clear – I didn't just need somewhere to go, somewhere to get me away from home. I needed company. I needed a few mates – not Daniel or anyone at the club, because that was part of the whole home thing – Jim Banks, my dad and all that. And not the likes of Matlock and Hughes either; they were just idiots. I needed someone normal.

Let's not waste time here, I needed someone like Kyle, and over the course of that detention, the idea of hanging out with him, in a hideout down by the river, didn't seem such a bad idea after all.

Gareth, on the other hand, was a waste of space. I didn't particularly like the idea of hanging out with him, but I didn't really have anything *against* him either.

The problem was, I was probably the last person in the world either of them would want to share a hideout with. I'm not saying that's not my own fault – after all, I'd pretty much threatened to kill the two of them. Even if I got the information out of Kyle, the chances of them ever going back there would be slim. I'd have a hideout, but I'd only have it to myself.

So I decided on a new strategy. I'd call it quits with Kyle, try to make up, get him talking. I didn't want to push him. I didn't want to prize the information out of him with too many questions. I wanted him to give it up, to talk about it freely and share the secret. I wanted him to invite me.

But he didn't. He didn't even hint at where they'd been. And the closer we got to home, the more frustrated I became. When it came to us going different ways, I came so close, so very close to just saying, 'Where's the hideout, Kyle? I heard Gareth mention it. Where were you hiding?'

But I didn't. I bit my tongue.

Kyle wasn't going to tell me, so there was only one thing I could do.

The next day was Saturday. It was a dry, bright and fairly warm day. I'd arranged to meet Gareth at the little road bridge that crossed the river at the village. Normally I'd get the bus down there, but I was all fired up about seeing the cave, so I filled my backpack with three cans of pop, four bags of crisps, biscuits, a Mars bar and a Twix, slung it over my shoulder and walked.

When I reached the bridge, Gareth was already there. He was leaning over the railings and looking into the water below. He had a backpack too, dumped on the ground beside him.

'You brought much?' I nasked.

'Yeah, all kinds. Crisps, pop, a big bag of nuts. I got some candles too. They'll make the place feel *really* creepy.'

'You brought matches?'

'Duh! I'm not going to bring candles and forget something to light them with.'

So we followed the narrow path alongside the river,

heading towards the viaduct and our cave. I told Gareth about the detention and all the details of the race to complete those lines, about how Alex had managed to corner me in the school, and then changed his mind and decided to call it quits.

Gareth came to a standstill. We were right outside the cave.

'I don't get it,' he said. 'He could have killed you.'

'Are you complaining that he didn't?'

'No. I'm just gob-smacked. I mean, he must have had an ulterior motive to do something like that.'

I shrugged. 'I don't think so. He said he couldn't remember why he wanted to get me, so it was time to call it quits.'

'You didn't remind him, did you?'

Oh cheers, Gareth! Am I that predictable?

'No!' I lied. 'We just walked home.'

'Together?'

'Yeah, he just wanted to chat.'

'Chat? What on earth can you "chat" about with someone like Alex Crow?'

'I don't know. Just this and that. He had a laugh about the chase the other day, about us climbing down by the viaduct to get away from him. He thought that was really brave. Stupid, but brave.'

Gareth suddenly looked serious and angry. 'What exactly did you tell him, Kyle?'

'Nothing. We were just talking.'

'Did he ask how we got away from him?'

'Yeah. At first I told him that we'd climbed back up the cliff, but he didn't believe me, so I just said we'd hid under the nettles. He laughed and said that was even braver than climbing down through the trees.'

'And that was it?'

'Yeah.'

'Nothing more?'

'Nothing more.'

Gareth had his hand on the ivy, but he suddenly pulled away and started looking about.

'What?' I asked. 'What's the matter?'

'There's something not right about this.'

'Hey, I'm just glad I lived to tell the tale. Come on. Let's get in before somebody sees us.' I parted the ivy and stepped inside the cave.

It was pitch black in there, and I expected Gareth to follow me inside.

He didn't. He remained outside, and I heard the fear in his voice as he muttered, 'Kyle?'

Even before I looked out, I knew something was wrong. My fears were confirmed with a voice I couldn't help but recognise.

'So that's your little hiding place.'

A terrible, sick feeling cut right through my entire body.

I parted the ivy, and there, standing on the path, chewing gum and grinning, was Alex Crow.

ALEX

You should have seen the look on Kyle's face when he saw me standing there. He didn't know whether to cry, faint or fill his kegs, and part of me was quite happy about it. After all, I'd been hanging around, waiting for them to turn up, for nearly half an hour.

I thought it would just be a case of sitting in the morning sun, gazing across the river and listening out for them. Sooner or later I'd hear them tramping up the road, laughing or chatting, and I'd sit up and get ready to make my move.

But it wasn't quite like that. I followed the path to that area beneath the viaduct at around nine o'clock, and already the place was full of noise. Every single bird in the local area must have flown there; the trees above were an assault of tweets and twitters. Kids passed by on bicycles, ringing bells, shouting at their dad to slow down, someone else came by with two dogs – one barking, the other jumping in and out of the water – and across the river, in a private residence, someone was racing around his grounds on the noisiest dirt bike in the world. The chance of simply hearing Kyle and Gareth as they approached was nigh on impossible.

In the end I moved to a spot where the area between the path and the river was wide, where there were enough bushes to crouch behind, but the view of the path itself was good. I knelt down and I waited.

Twenty minutes later, Kyle and Gareth came along chatting, laughing, and each carrying a backpack.

I slipped further into the bushes and kept my eyes peeled.

They were right in front of me. But instead of continuing along the road, they picked their way over the grass, towards the face of the cliff.

Slowly, quietly, I got to my feet to see what they were doing.

Gareth stopped right in front of the cliff face. For a moment, I thought he was going to try climbing up the ivy – a ridiculous thought – and then Kyle did something I could hardly believe. He moved a section of that ivy aside and stepped into the blackness beyond.

It was a cave, right there in the side of the cliff. I was so amazed at seeing what he'd done that I couldn't stop myself from stepping forward to get a better view.

Gareth must have sensed the movement, turned, and spotted me.

I had to say something, so I took another step forward. 'So that's your little hiding place.'

As Kyle stepped out from the cave, Gareth glared at him. 'You told him, didn't you? I can't believe you told him.'

'I didn't,' protested Kyle.

'Calm down, Gareth,' I said, stepping through the nettles. 'Kyle didn't tell me a thing.'

'So you just hid in the bushes hoping we'd come along?'

The hairs on my neck prickled. 'You being sarcastic?'

Gareth froze, but I gave him a friendly slap on the shoulder to show I didn't mean it, 'Give me a bit of credit, eh? It was obvious the two of you were hiding somewhere.' I stepped past Kyle and moved the ivy myself. All I could see was blackness beyond. It was certainly a cave, but it was a bloody big one.

'Careful with that,' said Kyle.

'What?'

'I just mean . . . be gentle with the ivy.'

'Don't tell me what to do, Kyle.' I felt the muscles in my shoulders tighten and almost told him I'd pull the lot down if I wanted, but instead I bit my tongue and reassured him, 'I was *going* to be careful. It's camouflage, isn't it?'

'Yeah.'

I looked into the cave again. 'So who's got the torch?'

'We forgot it,' said Gareth. 'We were just about to go back, weren't we, Kyle?'

'Erm, yeah.'

I gave out a loud sigh. 'How stupid do you two think I am? Give me that.' I snatched Gareth's bag from him and pulled it open. I was amazed at all the crap he'd managed to cram in there.

'Jeezus, Gareth. Looks like you've got half a shop in here. And look at this, right on the very top. A nice big torch!'

I grabbed it, chucked the bag back at Gareth and clicked the torch on. Without waiting for them to moan and complain,

I shone it into the cave and stepped inside.

I was immediately overcome with the size of the place. It was enormous.

'I really need to get back, Alex,' said Gareth. 'My dad will kill me if I don't bring the torch with me.'

'Calm down, will you? No one is going to kill anyone. I told Kyle last night that I'd call it quits, didn't I, Kyle? And I stand by my word; it's over. Finito. You got that?'

'Yeah, OK.'

'Good, so there's no need to make up stories about getting back home. You've both got bags with you; it's pretty clear you're planning to be here for a while, so why don't you get yourselves in here before someone spots you, eh? There's no point having a place like this if the rest of the world knows about it.'

They shuffled inside, letting the ivy close behind them. I shone the torch at their faces. They both looked terrified. The only thing I could do about that was to ignore it and hope they'd calm down.

I tried to keep the conversation going. 'You were hiding in here, eh?'

Kyle shrugged. 'Yeah.'

I pulled the torch away from them, looking about at the ceiling, at the walls and floor, feeling the cold air on my face. 'How long have you two known about this place?'

'Just since the other day,' said Kyle. 'I sort of fell inside.'

'Really?'

'Really.'

'I must have walked right past.'

'You did,' said Kyle. 'We saw you.'

163

I shone the torch back at them. There was a moment of tension, and Gareth looked ready to run, but I tried to ignore that too. I returned the light to the walls. 'It's an amazing find. Amazing. And you're dead right about that ivy. We'll have to be very careful with that. Once that comes down, it's game over.'

There was no response. The torchlight was strong enough that I could see them without shining the beam in their faces. It was clear what they were thinking. They were wondering if I was muscling in, if I was going to claim the place for myself. They didn't trust me.

I kept my tone light. 'What were you planning to do in here?'

'Nothing,' said Kyle. 'We just came to see if it was still here.'

I rolled my eyes. 'Don't treat me like an idiot, Kyle. Gareth has brought enough chocolate and crisps to keep the two of you alive for a month.' I shone the torch towards the entrance. 'So what else have you brought? Come on, you can tell me.'

They exchanged glances and looked uncomfortable.

'Look,' I said. 'You've got the best hideout in the country so you must have come here with *something* in mind.'

Again, I was faced with silence and discomfort.

'Oh, man,' I said, my voice slightly hushed. 'You weren't planning on kissing and stuff, were you?'

Kyle twisted his face. 'Fuck off!'

Immediately, his flare of anger melted into panic, fear.

I was quite impressed, and couldn't contain a laugh. 'I'm winding you up, Kyle.'

He looked uncertain, then managed a relieved smile. I think he'd shocked himself.

But a second later, he was looking uncomfortable again. He tried to say something, hesitated, and then started again. 'You're not going to tell anyone about this place, are you?'

I clicked my tongue and winked. 'I'm a psychopath, Kyle, not an idiot.'

Both of them looked stunned, so I added, 'I know what people say about me. It doesn't mean it's true. Well, not all of the time. Certainly not today. Gareth, what else you got in that bag?'

Gareth shrugged. 'Just some stuff. Nothing much.'

'He brought candles,' said Kyle. 'We thought we'd fix the place up, you know?'

'Yeah? Show me.'

With clear reluctance, Gareth pulled out crisps, biscuits, chocolate and then books.

'Books! Why the hell have you brought books?'

'It's just stuff,' said Gareth, still hunting. Finally he pulled out a candle. 'There.'

'And that's everything, is it?'

'That's everything.'

I looked down at the books on the ground. 'You two really know how to have a good time, don't you?'

'They're ghost stories,' said Kyle.

'Horror,' corrected Gareth.

I held up my hands and said, 'Let me get this right. You're going to sit down, light candles and read horror stories to each other? In a cave? With a torch?' I looked from one to the other, half expecting them to deny it. I felt like laughing. I *wanted* to laugh, but something inside held me back, and I found myself weighing it up, even pushing out my bottom lip and nodding. 'You know, that's not such a bad idea.' I glanced about at the space around us. 'In fact, this place will look pretty creepy once you get those candles going. How many did you bring?'

Gareth leaned into the bag and took out a second candle.

I paused, waiting for him to get the rest. When he didn't, the realisation hit home.

'Two. Is that all you've got? Two?'

'That's all we had in the kitchen drawer.'

'Two candles won't even light the walls in a place this size. Now if you had twenty, or thirty, *then* we'd be talking. We could make this place look fantastic, but two? For Christ's sake . . .' I trailed off and looked about. They had something here, the germ of a good idea. I felt like saying the place was wasted on them, but their ideas were on the right track. What we needed was . . . was . . .

And then it clicked.

'What this place needs is a fire. A real fire. A camp fire.'

Kyle looked about. 'There's not a lot to burn.'

'Are you kidding? There's half a forest just outside the door, stuff we can bring in. Branches, paper, litter – any old rubbish. Don't you two know anything about building a camp?'

'This is the first one we've found,' said Kyle.

'Listen, boys, the first thing any decent camp needs is a fire. I take it you've got matches – you can't have brought candles without matches.'

'Course we have,' said Gareth.

'OK then. Let's get to work, eh?'

There were several rocks lying here and there in that cave, especially towards the back. Most were small but there were a few boulders. I pointed to them. 'See those rocks. We can use the bigger ones to sit on. Spread them out, say one here, one there, one over there. Then collect some smaller stones and make a ring in the centre.'

'A ring?' said Gareth. 'What for?'

'For the fire, stupid. It keeps it all neat.' I grabbed hold of one of the larger rocks. 'Well come on then. Give me a hand shifting these.'

A moment later, we were all working together, pulling the larger rocks about the place. They were odd shapes and took a good deal of effort to move. They didn't roll as such, but if you could get a grip you could heave them over, and then over again, twisting them this way and that to steer them in the general direction. I did most of the heavy work, with Kyle coming a close second, while Gareth busied himself with the smaller stones to form a ring for the fire. When we finished, we sat down to examine our work.

Gareth wiped his brow with his sleeve. 'I'm worn out.'

'You?' said Kyle. 'It was me and Alex that did the hard graft.'

And with those words, I actually felt part of a gang, like I was one of the three rather than the lunatic on the sidelines.

'Gareth did his share too,' I said, looking at the circle of stones he'd created. 'That's a good size for a camp fire. Right, we'll take two minutes to get our breath back, then we can get some fuel, yeah?'

'Yeah,' said Gareth. 'If you say so.'

His words knocked me a little. It was like being back at square one. Once again I had to bite my lip. 'It'll be great.

I'm telling you, this place will look awesome once we get the fire going, eh?'

This time Gareth nodded. And he actually smiled.

'I'll make a start,' I said, and I got to my feet. 'Then we can hear some of those horror stories you've brought. OK?'

KYLE

As soon as we were back outside in the bright, warm sunlight, we began searching for things we could burn. Gareth moved over towards me. 'There is something all wrong about this. Don't you think?'

'I dunno.'

'Oh come on, Kyle. That's Alex Crow over there. Besides, it's going to be rubbish trying to tell stories with him cackling at every other line.'

'You don't think he'll be scared?'

'He'll just take the piss. You know he will. If we don't leg it now, we might not get another chance.'

'What about your stuff? It's still inside the cave. Are you going to leave it there?'

Gareth hadn't thought about this and looked all the worse for it. He glanced over his shoulder. 'If I have to, then yeah, I will.'

Alex was about five metres away, dragging a huge branch towards the cave. A thought occurred to me and I said, 'Ghost stories might not scare him, but what about your other stories? Those urban legends. They worked on Sean Matlock. He never said another word to you for the rest of that trip.'

Gareth sucked his lip, thinking. 'I don't know. Matlock was different.'

'He's not that different. They're both thugs. Come on, man. I really don't want to lose the cave. And I'm sure you don't want to lose your books.' I looked away and sighed. 'Maybe he'll be OK. You know? I mean, he was all right when we finished detention. He could have beaten me to a pulp if he wanted.' I flicked my eyes towards Alex. 'Take a look. It's not like he's sitting back and making us do what he says.'

Gareth wasn't happy but finally he gave in. 'If he starts getting weird, whether it's making jokes or threatening to belt us, then I'm off – even if that means leaving the books, the bags, the lot.'

•

It was clear that Alex had made fires before. He started by tearing newspaper up into little pieces, making a base. Then he snapped up the smallest, driest twigs and dropped them on top of the paper base. He covered the base with more paper, then more twigs and finally, right on top, bits of broken branch. To his right he had a small pile of all of the other stuff we'd collected, sweet wrappers, bits of cardboard packaging, hardboard – we were amazed at the amount of crap that was lying about so far from any houses.

Alex took a single match and struck it. Our eyes had become

used to the dark and the orange flare illuminated his face as he leaned forward. He cupped the burning match in his hands, lit the paper at one side, then the other.

I glanced at Gareth, but neither of us said a word. The newspaper curled, blackened and burned. Tiny flames came to life and grew, crackling through the twigs, causing the newspaper above to brown with the heat. At this point, Alex leaned further forward, so that his face was right up close, and began to gently blow into the base of the fire.

'What are you doing?' I asked.

Alex looked up and smiled. It wasn't a nasty smile, or anything, it simply said that I knew nothing about making fires.

'You have to nurture it,' he said. 'Treat it with a bit of care, otherwise the paper burns up, the fire goes out and you're back to square one.' He blew again, this time stronger, and again and again. There was a loud pop and a crackle. The fire was definitely taking, and I could feel the heat it was giving off. Even at this early stage, it lit the walls of the cave, creating shadows, black silhouettes of the three of us, moving and flickering on the orange walls. It gave the place an entirely different feel. We had light and heat in a place that had been so dark and cold. This was no longer just a hole in the side of a cliff. This was our place. Our cave. Our camp.

Gareth held up a piece of hardboard he'd found, painted white on one side, 'Will this burn?'

Alex shrugged, grabbed it, snapped it in two and chucked it on the fire. 'Anything will burn, so long as it's not soaked through.' He grabbed the sheet of soggy cardboard that I had been holding. 'Like this.'

'I thought the flames would dry it out,' I lied.

Alex shook his head and chucked another piece of hardboard on.

I couldn't see the smoke, but I could certainly smell it. It stunk to high heaven and I couldn't help coughing once or twice.

'How big are you going to make it?'

'You want to be able to read, don't you?'

'Yeah, but we don't need to roast a pig.' I coughed again. 'I think it's big enough.'

Alex sat back on his rock. He prodded the fire a couple of times with a long piece of branch and nodded with satisfaction, 'Good fire, that. Makes the place look homely.' He looked at Gareth. 'You think so?'

Gareth coughed and waved his hand in front of his face.

Alex grinned. 'You're not scared of a bit of smoke, are you?'

Both of us instantly replied, 'No.'

I felt foolish, and by the way Gareth was looking at the ground, so did he. But I probably read him wrong, because a moment later, he looked up and said, 'Just don't go making us become blood brothers or anything.'

'Why would anyone want to do that?' said Alex.

Gareth looked from Alex to me like we were stupid. 'Don't you two read the newspapers?'

As soon as he said that, the hairs on the back of my neck prickled with excitement, and a voice inside my head said, *here we go* . . .

'My dad does,' said Alex. 'So what?'

'You don't know what happened to those kids?'

'What kids?'

'The kids in the paper, just two weeks back. Oh, man. This will freak you out.' As if to mirror Alex, Gareth picked up his own bit of branch and gave the fire a poke. Tiny, pinpoint embers of orange light flew up, dying in mid-air. Gareth kept his eyes on the fire.

'These two lads, about the same age as us, they had a camp in the woods next to their house. They used to spend their days playing Cowboys and Indians, tracking each other through the woods, that kind of thing.' He looked up at us. 'One of the lads was obsessed with Red Indians and he'd read in some book that if they'd made a bond with someone, then they'd to do this thing, this ritual, right? They'd become blood brothers. Well this kid, he'd read all about it, and he thought he knew how, so him and his best mate, that's what they tried to do.'

Alex looked suspicious. 'They actually became blood brothers?'

'Yeah. And they did it just like the Indians used to. They cut the back of their hands and they put them together then tied them tight with garden twine.'

'What for?'

'To make sure the blood mixes, but it takes time. They had to sit like that for half an hour. Their hands were stinging like crazy, but they were best friends, and they genuinely thought that this would make them brothers, so they sat there and they put up with the pain. When the time was up, they untied the twine and bandaged up their wounds.'

'And that was it?' said Alex. He coughed and cleared his throat. 'They were blood brothers?'

'Yeah, but that's not the end of the story, because the next day they were supposed to go to school, but only one of them made it. When he asked the teacher where his friend was, she gave him the bad news . . .'

Gareth looked into the fire, his eyes squinting against the sting of the smoke, and whispered, 'He was dead.'

With the warmth of the fire on our fronts, the coldness of the cave seemed to close in tightly around us

Alex glanced at me, then he stared at Gareth. 'Dead?'

'That's right. He'd been rushed to hospital in the early hours of the morning. His family thought it was some kind of fever. And the doctors, they couldn't understand it. They said it was as though someone had given him a transfusion of the wrong blood type. His whole system was totally screwed up.'

'But what about his mate, the other lad?'

'Well, when the teacher told him the news, he suddenly realised why he felt so ill. He was sweating, burning up inside. The same thing was happening to him, see? He tried to tell his teacher, he tried to explain what had happened so the doctors would know what to do. But he couldn't get the words out. All he could do was hold his bandaged hand as the room began to spin . . . and then he fell. He was dead before he hit the floor.'

Alex just stared with wide grey eyes. For a moment he was silent. Then he gave a single clap of his hands and said, 'Awesome, Gareth. Truly awesome.'

What? I couldn't believe this . . . He was laughing. Alex Crow was actually laughing at one of Gareth's best stories yet.

But to make it worse, Gareth was laughing along with him. The smoke caught his breath and he coughed and spluttered, saying, 'You liked that?'

I couldn't understand why Gareth didn't care, why he wasn't insisting it was true. By the way he was laughing, he clearly *enjoyed* the fact that Alex wasn't fooled. Alex grabbed another few bits of wood and litter from the small pile and dumped them on the fire. 'Yeah, that was pretty good,' he said, 'But I can match it.'

Gareth looked impressed, but also cynical. He managed to control his coughing, folded his arms in a challenging pose and said, 'Yeah? Come on then.'

Alex sniffed and wiped the smile from his face. 'OK, so there was this bloke and his girlfriend, driving across the moors one night. They were in the middle of nowhere when they ran out of petrol, just as the news came on the radio, telling everyone to lock all doors and windows . . .'

I couldn't believe it. I had never imagined that Gareth and Alex could have anything in common, and yet here they were, exchanging scare stories like best mates.

I sat there, I listened and I even laughed, but inside I was chewed up and churning. This was *our* place; mine and Gareth's. The whole idea of them getting along and me sitting on the sidelines made me feel sick. In fact, as I thought about it, I really did feel sick – *physically* sick. Dizzy too, and beside me, while Alex told his tale, Gareth was finding it increasingly difficult to clear his throat.

'You OK?' I asked.

Alex shushed me. 'He's fine. Listen, right, because the bloke had to look for help, so he left her alone in the car . . .' and he continued his story.

But Gareth wasn't fine. He started leaning forward, coughing harder.

I looked towards the entrance. Earlier, we could see light filtering in through the ivy. I could hardly see a thing now and my eyes were stinging like crazy.

I stood up. 'I think we should get some air in here.'

Alex coughed and spat into the fire. 'Sit down, Kyle. This is the best part.'

Now I was on my feet, I felt even worse. It was like the smoke was suddenly thicker.

'No. I need some air.'

Next to me, Gareth almost choked in order to say, 'Me too.'

Alex was on his feet. 'Sit down, Kyle. It's just a bit of smoke.'

It wasn't just a bit of smoke though. It was much, much thicker nearer the roof of the cave and it caught Alex off guard. He almost doubled over, retching, his arm across his mouth. 'Jeezus.'

I grabbed Gareth by the arm, helping him to his feet. 'Get up. Come on, man, we're going outside.'

Alex was coughing his guts up, but he was shaking his head and holding a hand out.

I should have pushed past him. I should have kept hold of Gareth's arm, pushed past Alex and run for the exit, but I paused, and in that moment of hesitation, Gareth slumped. He fell backwards and landed on his side with a thump.

'Gareth!'

Alex looked terrified. 'Holy shit.'

I slapped Gareth on the arm and shouted his name. His eyes were half open, but there was no reaction.

As I grabbed one arm, hooking it over my shoulder, I shouted at Alex, 'We've got to get him out.'

Alex froze for a moment, then he jumped over the fire and tried to give me a hand, but even together, we could barely lift Gareth.

Standing up, I got another lungful of smoke, immediately coughing and spluttered, 'We'll have to drag him.'

But I couldn't stop coughing; I couldn't get my breath at all and I lost my grip on Gareth's arm.

Alex barked at me, 'Kyle. Get up.'

I tried, but ended up leaning on Gareth, holding up a hand to say, give me a second.

Alex ran towards the entrance and started tearing down chunks of the ivy.

I could see the light from outside, fighting its way through the blue haze, and I could hear Alex shouting and yelling. There was buzzing in my ears. Buzzing all around, in my body, legs, arms, lips.

'Come on, Gareth. Wake up . . .'

And then I was kneeling next to him.

Alex was gone.

The light faded to black and, like Gareth, I slipped into unconsciousness.

ALEX

It was the smoke. There's always smoke when you make a fire. Sometimes it blows in your face and you cough, sometimes it blows the other way and you don't. Part and parcel of fires – it goes with the territory. But when I stood up, it felt like it was ten times stronger and it took the wind right out of me.

And then Gareth keeled over.

We tried to get him out, the two of us. I grabbed one arm, Kyle grabbed the other, but he was a dead weight. I couldn't believe how heavy he was. When Kyle dropped down, it was even worse. There was no way I could get him out on my own.

Maybe if I got Kyle out. He was a fraction of the weight. But I couldn't even do that. I needed to breathe. I needed fresh air, but I didn't want to leave them there, so I ran to the entrance and began tearing at the ivy. I screamed for help as I tugged and ripped, but the ivy was tougher than I thought and all I got were handfuls of leaves. At the same time, the smoke was pouring out through every gap I made, and I ended up choking once again.

I coughed my guts up and yelled as loud as I could, 'HELP! Someone, HELP!'

Earlier on, when I'd been waiting for Kyle and Gareth to turn up, everyone and his bloody dog had passed by. There must be someone.

I staggered towards the path, falling to my knees just as I got there. And I saw them, two figures coming this way. The bloke looked so big that I thought I must be hallucinating. I guess he was a bodybuilder or something, and he had this tiny, skinny little girl by his side.

The whole world started to spin. The last thing I remember is falling to my knees, puking all over myself.

KYLE

'Kyle.'

I recognised the voice.

I opened my eyes, squinted at the brightness, and closed them again.

'Kyle.'

I tried a second time. I was in bed in a small room with white walls. There was a colourful, cartoon border pasted high up, close to the ceiling. My mum was sitting by the side of the bed, leaning towards me. I felt a mask across my face.

'It's all right, Kyle. Just oxygen. And there's a drip in your arm but nothing to worry about.'

A nurse looked in through the open doorway. 'Oh! Awake, are we?' She approached the bed. 'Your poor lungs won't know what hit them.'

I tried to speak, but instead began to cough.

The nurse grabbed a grey, cardboard bowl from behind

the bed. 'Sit up, love.' She handed me the bowl, pulled the mask from my head and rubbed my back with hard, vigorous movements. My next cough gripped, erupting in a fat, meaty, splat of mucus, snot and slime right in the centre of the bowl. White, yellow and, to my horror, red.

'A little bit of blood in there too, eh? Don't you worry about that, Kyle. You're on the mend. You need another?'

I did. And another, and another. By the end, just breathing in seemed to crush my whole chest.

She gave me some painkillers, flushing them directly into my drip tube.

'You're doing a lot better than you were before.'

'Before?'

My mum leaned forward. 'You woke up when you first came in. You mumbled something about ivy and how the camp was ruined. Then you went back to sleep.'

The nurse replaced my mask. 'You should get some peace and quiet in here. You're off the main ward. Although, I think there's someone who would like a few words.'

She left and a man stepped into the room, closing the door behind him. He was tall and broad, wearing a shirt and tie but no jacket. He smiled as he came in, but he had an air of authority that made me uncomfortable.

'Good morning, Kyle,' he said. 'You look a bit more lucid today.'

'Sorry?'

'You don't remember me, do you?'

I shook my head.

The man laughed. 'You were away with the fairies yesterday.'

I just stared at him.

181

'So how do you feel?'

'Like shit.'

My mum looked shocked. 'Kyle!'

'That's all right. I'm sure that's a fairly accurate description.'

'Are you the doctor?' I had a feeling he wasn't.

'No, Kyle. I'm a policeman. Detective Sergeant Miller. *DS* Miller to my friends.' He grinned like this was his best joke. 'I'm here to ask a few questions.'

I tried to move the oxygen mask but DS Miller held up a hand. 'It's OK, I can understand you fine. Just take your time and tell me what you remember.'

I tried to think back, but there was nothing. Nothing at all. I knew I was in hospital, but I didn't know why.

'The cave,' prompted my mum. 'Do you remember the cave?'

And there it was. Click. I remembered finding the cave. I remembered Alex Crow chasing us. I remembered . . .

'The fire.'

'Yes,' DS Miller nodded. 'There was a fire. Good. Just concentrate on that for a moment. Try to recall who made it.'

It took a few seconds before I managed to say, 'Gareth,' at which point my mum turned away and I heard an intake of breath.

DS Miller looked concerned. 'Gareth had the matches?'

'Yes.'

'So he made the fire?'

I couldn't remember. And then, 'No. Gareth . . . Gareth brought candles. We were only going to light candles. Alex wanted the fire.'

'So Alex made the fire?'

'No. I think . . . We all helped. We brought stuff in from outside. Twigs. Paper. Just stuff.'

'Good. You're doing great, Kyle. Do you remember it getting smoky in there?'

'Yeah. I can remember it hurting my eyes. We kept coughing.'

'Why didn't you leave?'

I tried to think, but there was still nothing there. It was like my mind had been wiped clean. It was horrible.

'I don't remember.'

'Do you remember *wanting* to leave?'

'I don't know. I don't remember.' I looked at my mum for some kind of support, but she was ashen white and seemed to be siding with the policeman.

Then, without any kind of warning, and with tears in her eyes, my mum seemed to explode. 'What were you *doing* in such a stupid, stupid place? What were you doing in there, Kyle? And to start lighting fires . . . What were you *thinking*?'

Something else seemed to click into place. 'I think . . . I think we were telling stories. Why? What happened?'

'You very nearly killed yourselves, that's what happened.'

I had never seen her so angry.

DS Miller explained, 'The foliage covering the entrance to the cave acted like a screen door. I don't know what you boys were burning in there, but something or other was giving off some nasty toxins. Enough to knock you out.'

'But we got out, didn't we? So . . . we must have crawled out.'

The policeman shook his head. 'I'm afraid not, Kyle. You and Gareth were found inside the cave. Alex was found on the path nearby. That's why we need to know exactly what happened inside that cave; why Alex managed to get out, but you and Gareth did not.'

'But. We're here. Aren't we?' I could hear the panic in my own voice. I didn't know what they were trying to say, but I got the feeling that something was very wrong. 'How come I'm here?'

'You were dragged out,' said my mum.

'A young man walking along the river with his sister saw Alex collapse on the path. The girl spotted the smoke and her brother went to investigate. He was the one who dragged you out. You first. Gareth second.'

'So Gareth is here too?'

DS Miller took a deep breath. 'I'm afraid Gareth is ill. Very ill indeed.'

'He's in Intensive Care,' said my mum.

'Which is why it is so important that you tell us everything you remember. There's no reason to hold anything back, Kyle. No reason to be scared.'

At that, something seemed to fall into place and I muttered, 'Scared?'

My mum sat up. 'What were you scared of, Kyle? Did Alex make you stay in that cave?'

I shook my head. 'No. We were going to scare Alex. Gareth was, with his stories. He was telling stories . . .'

'So why were you in the cave?' asked Miller.

'It was a camp. A hideout.'

'I see.'

My mum put a hand on the bed, 'But you weren't friends with this boy, were you? This other boy?' There was panic

184

in her eyes, and she glanced at Miller before saying, 'You've never done anything like this before, have you, Kyle? You've never made fires. Neither has Gareth.'

DS Miller spoke in a careful, clear tone. 'Kyle?' he asked. 'Is there anything else you remember about being in the cave? Anything at all? Because . . . if it was anything more than a game, just the three of you messing around, if . . .' He glanced at my mum.

She was glaring at him, fury emblazoned on her face and interrupted, '. . . if this *Alex* made you stay in there against your wishes, then you have to say something, Kyle. It's very important.'

I didn't know what to say. As far as any solid memories were concerned, my mind was still blank, but I had several thousand questions.

'Is Gareth going to be OK? Can I see him?'

DS Miller held up a hand. 'For now, just keep focussed on what happened.'

I tried, but ended up shaking my head. 'I can't remember any more.' Then I looked at DS Miller directly. 'How did Alex get out? Why didn't he pass out? And why didn't *he* drag us out?'

DS Miller didn't answer. His face was grim. He was waiting for me to say something else, but what else was there to say?

I looked at my mum for some kind of answer. 'Mum?'

She put her hand on my knee and said, 'That's what DS Miller is trying to find out, Kyle. He wants to know why you two were left inside.'

ALEX

My dad was furious that a copper had interviewed me without his consent. I was feeling sick and weak, but I still managed to say, 'So why don't you put a complaint in?'

His eyes were wild, and he'd spent every moment in my side room biting his nails to the quick. 'Don't get clever with me, boy. Just tell me what he was asking. What did he say?'

'He was asking about the cave. That's all.'

He spat out a piece of nail. 'Words. I want the actual *words*. What did he say?'

I really couldn't be bothered with this. My mam was sitting at the far side of the room, shaking her head and occasionally mumbling to herself, which was almost as bad. Both were doing my head in. I was ready to press the nurse call button and ask for the two of them to be kicked out.

I took a deep breath and answered my dad's question. 'He asked me who started the fire – who had the matches.'

'And?'

'Gareth had the matches. I started the fire.'

'You said what?'

'I told him that I started the fire, so what?'

He was up on his feet again.

'Idiot,' he said. He'd been up and down all morning. In the chair one moment, at the window the next, checking the door, back in his chair. Never still, and never quiet. 'Fucking idiot!'

'Will,' said my mum, 'there's doctors about.' She looked at me. 'Maybe you made a mistake, Alex. You could tell him that. When he comes back, tell him you made a mistake.'

That didn't wash with my dad. 'You've accepted liability,' he snapped. 'That's what you've done. You've said it was your fault. Bloody *idiot*. You should have said you couldn't remember. What have I always told you? Eh? When it comes to uniform, what have I always said?'

'To keep my mouth shut.'

'That's right.' He leaned over the bed. 'You keep your mouth *shut*. You act dumb. You act like you know nothing. If it's so important, let them find out for themselves. That's what they get paid for. What you don't do is go offering them answers on a plate.'

I was amazed to hear my mam speak up for me. 'Boys are always lighting fires, Will. Besides, it wasn't even Alex's matches, so those other boys, they were going to have a fire anyway. What difference does it make who lit it?'

My dad turned like he'd been hit with 10,000 volts of electricity. 'What difference? Are you stupid? The difference is that they'll want to ask him more questions. They'll come to the house. They'll delegate some damn social worker or something to find out if he's a potential arsonist, they'll keep a file on him, and not just him, but us – you and me – to see if we're the root of his problems, and they won't leave us alone until they're satisfied one way or the other. That's the difference. Jesus!'

For once my mam didn't back down. She lowered her eyes, but she didn't bite her tongue as she usually would. 'I just don't see why you're so worked up about it, that's all.'

Before my dad could go off in another rant, I spoke up. 'I know why. I understand.'

My dad had looked ready to give my mam a back-hander, but when he heard those words he froze and stared at me with unmasked disbelief.

'What did you say?'

I wanted to keep cool, but the moment was broken by a bout of coughing. My mam didn't exactly get to her feet, but she leaned forward – the next best thing – and asked if I was all right, if I needed the nurse.

'He's fine,' said my dad, still staring at me.

I cleared my throat, got my breath back and lay heavily on my pillow. I looked back at my dad. I was feeling thoroughly ill, but I knew he couldn't touch me. I even smiled.

'I know why you don't want those people round our house,' I said. 'Poking their noses in, asking questions.'

His eyes were burning. I had no doubt how much he wanted to drag me out of that bed and give me the hiding of my life, but he said nothing, he did nothing, so I carried on.

'Gareth is really ill. That's what the copper said.'

'He would. Trying to make you feel guilty.'

'Guilty for what? I didn't do anything wrong. We all helped find stuff to burn and we all sat round it together. He told me because Gareth is in Intensive Care.'

My dad just sneered. 'He told you to get under your skin.'

I could feel myself getting riled. I'd seen a different side to Gareth in that cave. Having my dad sneer like that made my fingers clench. I decided to wipe that smile right off his face.

'He thinks I left them,' I said. 'Miller. He thinks I left Kyle and Gareth in that cave. I told him the truth. I tried to pull down the ivy. I tried to let fresh air in, and I went for help, because there was no way I could carry them out on my own.'

My dad looked unsure. 'And that's what you told him, is it?'

'Yeah. But he didn't believe me. He didn't believe a word I told him. He thinks I lit the fire, saw them pass out and legged it. And that's why he'll come to the house, to see if I've got the makings of a murderer.' I couldn't help a small grin myself. 'What do you think, dad? You think I've got that streak in me?'

I couldn't believe I'd taken things so far. And by the look on his face, neither could he.

He pointed a shaking finger right at my face. 'Sort out this attitude, boy. When you get home, we're going to have a long talk about a few things. You understand?'

KYLE

Whenever I asked to see Gareth, I got the same reply, 'Intensive Care is for immediate family only. Sorry.'

I tried three different nurses. None of them budged. But I wasn't going to give up.

I was having no luck with the nurses, so I tried the doctor.

As soon as the words were out of my mouth, my mum tutted and whispered, 'Kyle, you know you can't.'

The doctor gave a friendly enough smile, but sided with everyone else, his only reason being, 'Your friend is still quite poorly. He needs rest.'

But I pushed it. 'Can't I just see him? He's my best friend. I've known him since I was three.'

That was something Alex Crow couldn't say. And it seemed to have some effect.

'Since you were three?'

'They're very close,' said my mum, finally backing me up.

·

I thought I was getting used to the smell of hospital, and of the sight of tubes and monitors. I was brought back down to earth with a thump when I stepped into the Intensive Care Unit. I couldn't *count* the amount of machines surrounding Gareth.

Monitors showed graphs of his heartbeat. There were infusion units, syringe pumps, tubes and clamps and god-knows what else.

A ventilator stood to the left of his bed, just where a bedside table should have been, giving out a deep hiss, followed by a pause, and then a high hiss and a pause. On each deep hiss, the tubes linking Gareth to the machine would twitch with the air pressure and Gareth's chest would rise. On each high hiss, his chest would relax.

'Why don't you tell him you're here?'

I nearly jumped. There was a nurse at my side, smiling as though there was nothing unusual about so many machines.

'Why don't you tell him you're here,' she said again, 'and that you've come to visit.'

I felt nervous. I felt silly. I felt like I'd been here before. Memories of my brother in his incubator, the feeling of being so completely out of place.

I stepped closer, and now I could see Gareth's face.

He looked as though he was sleeping. A tiny bead of saliva threatened to dribble from the corner of his mouth. The nurse, without making a big deal of the matter, dabbed it away with a tissue.

I heard a noise from behind. I'd almost forgotten that my

mum was in here with me. I knew she was crying and trying to cover the sound, but I couldn't take my eyes off Gareth.

'Is he going to be OK?' I asked.

'We're doing everything we can.'

She hadn't answered my question.

'How long will he be like this?'

'Hopefully, not too long. He just needs time to rest, for his body to repair itself.'

His body to repair *itself*? I thought it was the doctors who did the repairing.

I didn't get this. What was wrong? Why was he so much worse than me?

The nurse put her hand on my shoulder. 'It's probably best to keep your visit short. I wouldn't expect there to be much of a change for the next day or so. But I'm sure that Gareth knows you're here.' She paused and smiled. 'Would you like to say goodbye before you leave?'

I stepped forward, touched Gareth's hand and muttered, 'See you later, man.'

No reaction. The only movement was Gareth's chest, pushed up by another hiss of the ventilator.

•

I was OK when I left the Intensive Care Unit but as I walked the corridor of my own ward everything felt wrong. My legs, suddenly fizzy and weak. Pins and needles in my hands, the floor stretching, my heart rate going like a machine gun. I stumbled, felt for the wall and slipped down to the floor.

The next thing I remember is sitting on the bed in my own side room. There was a nurse in front of me, holding my hands, my mum in the background demanding to know what was going on.

'Slow your breathing,' said the nurse. 'Kyle. Try to calm down. You're hyperventilating, that's why you feel so bad.'

My head was spinning. The pins and needles had spread to my lips.

She squeezed my hand. 'That's it. Just slow down. Breathe slowly.'

My mum looked petrified, but she came closer, touching my arm.

'It's OK, pet. I think it was all a bit too much for you.'

ALEX

I wasn't supposed to see Kyle. DS Miller pretty much spelled it out to me.

'It would be better if you both had time to rest and recover,' he'd said. His voice was friendly, but his eyes were firm. 'I'm sure you understand.'

'Does that include Gareth?' I asked.

He didn't reply, he just looked at me like I should know better.

So I was mostly stuck on my own. My dad never returned after his first visit. When my mam came, she'd bring a couple of magazines, a bag of crisps, a bar of chocolate, then go through the same questions: had the doctors said anything about me coming home, and had I heard about the other boys? After that, she'd make some excuse and leave.

I tried watching TV but my mind kept drifting back to Kyle, and why Miller wanted us apart. I thought back to when he'd interviewed me. He had asked the same questions over and over: 'why did you leave them?', 'why didn't you at least try to drag Kyle out?', 'what made you so sure you'd find help?'

He thought I'd tried to leg it. He hadn't come out and said it, but that's what he was thinking, and if anything my dad says about coppers is right, he'd have been telling Kyle that very thing.

Would Kyle believe him? Or would he remember what really happened?

The more I thought about it, the more I realised I had to speak to Kyle.

I had to know for sure.

•

I tried to be casual as I walked past Kyle's room. The door was open a crack. I could see that someone was on the bed and I could hear the TV, so I guessed Kyle was in there alone.

I looked back towards the nurse's station. One nurse was busy on the phone, the others were elsewhere.

No one would see me if I slipped into the room but what was I going to say to him? I mean, should I just say, 'Hi,' and see what he'd come back with? Nah. Too risky. What if he just told me to get lost or, worse, pressed the nurse call button?

So how about, 'Hey, Kyle. How you feeling?' Or should I ask about Gareth? Kyle was bound to know what was going on with him.

The sound of movement inside the room caused me to jump. He was getting off the bed.

For some reason, I found myself walking away.

•

Back in my own room, I tried to come to my senses. I mean, what the hell was I scared of? So what if he pressed the nurse call button. They wouldn't respond immediately. And what about him not wanting to talk? That was just as dumb. All I had to do was ask him. Ask him what Miller had said, tell him what had really happened. He'd listen, because he'd want to know.

But I didn't get up again. I sat in the chair in the corner of my room and switched channels on that TV. I don't know how long I stayed like that. It must have been a while because I was there until the doctor came round mid-afternoon. He told me I was fit enough to go home. The nurse looked all cheery, smiled and told me she'd phone my mother to come get me.

Whoopee do.

I opened the bedside cabinet, looked at my clothes all folded up, waiting for the off.

If my mam got the bus here, I'd be out in an hour. If my dad gave her a lift, it'd be less.

I picked up my jeans.

'Guess it's now or never.'

KYLE

A voice at the door said, 'How you doing?'

I looked up to see Alex dressed in jeans, trainers and a T-shirt.

I tried to sound calm. 'You look like you're leaving.'

'Just got the all-clear. Thought I'd come and say bye, you know?'

There was a moment of silence. I felt like telling him to go away, leave me alone, but I could feel questions bubbling away. I wanted to ask him so many things, about the cave, about what had happened, why he'd left us, but the words didn't come.

Alex shifted on his feet, moved a step forward and asked, 'What about you? You going home soon?'

I shrugged. 'Maybe tomorrow.'

'I've heard he's in Intensive Care. Gareth, I mean. I've heard he's pretty bad.'

I felt a twinge of anger, and almost mentioned that I'd seen him.

I decided against it. 'Yeah. I think he's going to be in for a while.'

There was an uncomfortable moment with neither of us speaking.

Alex asked, 'You seen that copper?'

He was trying to sound casual, I could tell, but there was a definite edge to his question.

'Yeah,' I replied. 'Just once.'

'Me too. Kept asking me the same stupid questions.'

I didn't know what to say. For some reason I blurted out, 'I told him we were just messing around, telling stories – just like we did.'

Alex looked at me, his pale-grey eyes giving nothing away. He looked like he was going to say something else, but before he got the chance, my mum appeared behind him, a bag in one hand, two sandwiches in the other. Alex must have heard her footsteps and he glanced behind.

Then looked back at me. 'I'll see you around, eh?'

As I watched him go, I wondered if I should have said something else, if I should have asked him more. That was when I noticed the puzzled frown on my mum's face.

'What's up?'

She looked round, watching Alex walk down the corridor. 'That boy . . .'

I lay back on the bed. 'Yeah, that was Alex. Why?'

She paused for a second then shook her head. 'Nothing.'

But she still had that frown.

ALEX

My dad was waiting outside in the car.

As I climbed in and sat on the back seat, he looked at me through the rear-view mirror. 'How are you feeling?'

I was ready for an argument, so it took me a moment to collect my thoughts.

'Better,' I replied. 'I'm not one hundred per cent, but I'm getting there.'

He started the car. 'Champion. Best take it easy though. No need to go rushing back to school. Take a few days off, eh?'

My mam nodded, adding, 'The doctors said lots of rest.'

'You take all the time you need, son,' my dad said, and we pulled out of the car park, away from the hospital.

I must admit, I was taken aback by this. Not just at his concern, but the fact that he called me 'son', instead of the more usual 'boy'.

But then he screwed it all up.

'The last thing you need right now is those teachers giving you the third degree.'

KYLE

It was good to be home.

When the doctor gave me the all-clear, he said I was fit to go back to school. My mum said it was up to me, but I didn't feel ready. Not just yet.

I went upstairs, lay on my bed and stared up at the ceiling.

The only sound was a slight shuffling coming from the vivarium. The scorpion was busying itself in its boring, predictable way. Normally this didn't bother me, but right then, it infringed enormously on my need for peace. Sounds that were usually too quiet to hear were suddenly scratching and scraping inside my head. In the end I was forced to get up and see what the wretched thing was doing.

The sawdust and soil mixture that formed the base of the scorpion's home was about two inches deep. There was a piece of curved bark in there. The scorpion hid underneath stuff but every now and then it scraped the soil about, digging burrows, better hiding places. That's about it. That's all it ever did.

And yet Gareth was transfixed by it. He was always saying that one day he'd pick it up, but I kept warning him off. So much for being docile. The thing I'd been sold must have had faulty wiring or something because every time I went near it, its tail would curl tight and its pincers would lift up ready to fight.

I found myself wondering what would happen if I took a different approach. What if I put my hands *behind* it?

I removed the top of the vivarium and peered inside.

The scorpion twitched, but didn't go into fight mode.

I reached my hands in, keeping them close to the sides of the glass.

The scorpion stayed perfectly still.

I moved my hands down slowly, carefully, until I shuffled them into the sawdust and soil mix. The scorpion twitched several times and then stood still. I kept moving, shifting sawdust and soil away, until finally the sides of my hands touched together.

I was, in effect, actually holding the scorpion for the very first time.

Next, I gradually lifted the whole chunk off the floor with the scorpion sitting on top until my hands were above the vivarium and I was face to face with my pet.

There was a good inch of sawdust and soil between its feet and the palms of my hands. I started to wriggle my fingers. The scorpion lifted its pincers high, defensive, and I froze. It shifted its footing, but relaxed, so I started to wriggle my fingers again, allowing more soil and sawdust to fall until all I had in my hands was the black, shiny scorpion itself.

I had never looked at it so closely and for the first time I realised that it was more of a deep, dark green than pure black, and there were tiny details I'd never noticed before. It was a complicated, ugly creature, but it was fascinating too. And to be finally holding it in my own hands was as thrilling as it was terrifying. All I could hear was my own breath, my own pulse, my own heartbeat.

Downstairs the telephone rang, but I didn't flinch. I just stood there, holding my scorpion, wondering what the hell I was trying to prove and what I was going to do next.

And then a voice to my left said, 'You're a braver man than me.'

I snapped my head round and found myself staring at Gareth. He was standing right next to me, fully dressed with a big stupid grin on his face.

'Gareth!' I cried.

Whether it was the sound of me speaking, or my sudden movement, the scorpion sensed danger. It gripped my skin with its pincers and its tail shot forward, piercing the skin just below my thumb.

I screamed out, but the thing had nipped its pincers tight and wasn't about to let go. It stung again and again before I managed to shake it back into its vivarium. It landed angrily on its feet and immediately ran for cover.

The pain was intense. Absolutely, incredibly, one hundred and fifty per *cent* intense. The book said it was supposed to be no worse than a bee sting. Well the book was full of shit because I'd been stung by a bee the year before and it was nothing compared to the red-hot needles driving into every single point the scorpion had hit. I wanted to jump and run and crouch down all at the same time. I squeezed the wounds and shook my hands and bit them and ended up crouching down on the floor.

I managed to pull myself together enough to look about the room, but there was no sign of Gareth. The door was closed, just as it had been ever since I came in.

The pain was driving me mental – pulsing, jabbing – and I was desperate to put ice on it or something, so I pulled open my door.

As I reached the bottom of the stairs I heard my mum say goodbye and put down the phone. I expected her to ask what all the shouting was about, but she didn't. She didn't even turn round.

'Mum? Who was on the phone?'

I walked closer.

'Mum?'

Finally, she turned. She seemed to be weighing things up. 'That was Gareth's mum,' she said.

The pain was still jabbing, but suddenly it didn't seem so important. 'Gareth?'

'She was asking if you'd like to go and see him.'

I think I stood there, just looking at her for ages before it sunk in. 'So . . . he's OK?'

She only gave me the smallest, slightest shake of her head.

ALEX

If my dad had been a little jumpy in the hospital, he nearly died when an unmarked car pulled up outside our house and DS Miller got out.

My dad whirled round and pointed at my mam. 'Get upstairs.'

'Don't be daft, Will. He might want a cup of tea.'

'Tea?' my dad's face transformed to painted joy. 'Oh, I'll go and buy some biscuits too, eh? Make him nice and comfy and see if he'll stay for dinner.' His scowl returned. 'Just get upstairs and keep your mouth shut.'

She gave a huff, but did as she was told.

'What about me?' I asked, half expecting to be ordered out the back door.

'You? You just sit still and watch what you say, got it?'

'Why did you send my mam upstairs?'

'Because she speaks out of turn, that's why. She doesn't

think before opening her mouth, does she?'

When the doorbell rang my dad ordered me to open it, then he picked up his paper and sat down.

The policeman greeted me with a smile. 'Hello, Alex, good to be home?' Without being asked, he stepped inside.

My dad called out from the front room, 'Who is it, Alex?'

Miller took a good look at me. 'Shouldn't your dad be answering the door? I thought you would be resting, not running errands.'

He walked past me and stepped into the front room.

'Mr Crow,' he said, acknowledging my dad.

My dad didn't get up. He was sitting so low in that chair that it looked like the seat was swallowing him. His hand was tapping on his knee as he forced a sarcastic smile. 'A home visit, is it?'

'I just came out to ask young Alex a couple of questions,' said Miller. His eyes locked on mine. 'I wondered if you'd remembered anything else about the cave, Alex. In light of recent events, things have taken a more serious turn.'

I could almost hear my dad flinch. 'Serious?'

DS Miller continued, 'The boy in Intensive Care. He's in a coma. His poor mother is inconsolable. The doctors and nurses are doing all they can, but . . .' He shrugged. 'So I wondered, Alex, if you had any more information. Best to get it all out now because if things get any worse . . . well, if that happens, we'll be in a different situation altogether. You understand what I'm saying, Alex?'

I tried to answer, but my voice cracked.

A coma? That was bad. Was that like brain-dead or something?

'Is Gareth going to die?'

'His situation is very serious, Alex. That's all I know.' He gave a sigh and a slight shake of his head. 'In retrospect, it's amazing that you're not in there with him. It so easily could have been all three of you.'

Not me. I got out. But it could have been Kyle.

Kyle could be lying in there.

I felt a stab of guilt. It wasn't like I wanted Gareth to be stuck in there, it was just . . . ah fuck it, I don't know.

'So anyway . . .' Miller opened a notebook and sat down. 'Do you mind going over events for me, just one more time?'

•

When Miller finally left, my dad exploded. 'What did I tell you? Eh? I said they'd be back, didn't I? Didn't I say that?'

'He came to tell me Gareth could die.'

'Yes, and he used it as a weapon, to try and break you.' He got to his feet and came over. 'You don't get it, do you? They don't stop. They *never* stop, and they'll use anything to get what they want.'

A surge of anger in my gut shot me to my feet and I heard myself shout, 'He came to tell me I nearly killed someone. Have you any idea how that feels?'

I was staring straight back at him and I could see him getting angrier and angrier. His eyes were wide. His face was red. I was ready for him to take a swing at me. He'd lift his arm over his head and take a wide slap at the side of my head, and I'd block it with ease. But instead, his arms shot out like pistons – bang! Right in my chest, shoving me backwards, back into my chair.

What shocked me wasn't the move, but that it knocked the wind right out of me – something that would never happen. And it was no fluke. He knew exactly what he was doing, where I was weakest.

Before I had time to recover, he snatched up his paper and left the room. The door slammed and I heard him stomping up the stairs shouting, 'Bloody fool. You just don't get it, do you?'

A few seconds later I heard him screaming at my mam.

Enough was enough. I got up, winced at the jolt from my ribs, and ran upstairs after him.

They were in the bedroom. He didn't have his hands on her, but she was up against the bedroom mirror and his finger was pointed right in her face.

I stepped into the room. 'Leave her alone.'

His eyes were blazing and he looked ready to fight.

I stepped forward but as I took a breath to tell him to back off, I felt pain cut right across my chest. It was much stronger than before and I buckled.

My mam rushed towards me. 'Alex?'

I put a hand out to keep her off. 'I'm OK. I'm fine.' I took slow, careful breaths, keeping the pain at bay.

'You're still not well,' she said. 'You shouldn't rush upstairs like that.'

I held my dad's stare. 'Good job I did though, isn't it?'

KYLE

It was strange walking through the foyer of the hospital. Up there, back on my ward, someone else would be in my bed, some other kid with some other illness.

Not Gareth though. He'd be in the same bed.

My mum walked next to me. 'Are you sure you're OK with this? It was such a big shock to you last time.'

'I'll be fine. Will Gareth's mum be there?'

'Probably. But she doesn't mind. She *wants* you to visit him.'

I nodded. 'Yeah.'

'Maybe a familiar voice . . . you know?'

I nodded. We were at the lifts. 'Yeah. I know.'

We stepped into the lift along with about four other people. I hoped they were all visitors. I didn't like the idea of being in a sealed metal box with people carrying diseases from one floor to the next. I tried to be subtle and stepped back. It wasn't as though I was being rude – there was room in that lift for twenty or more. It was massive, certainly bigger than your average lift, so I made out I was just stretching my legs and moved to the back.

The bell chimed and the doors opened. No one left, but waiting outside was a full-sized hospital bed.

So that was why they were so big. I felt a bit stupid really, it seemed so obvious.

Everyone moved back, shuffling up next to me to make room for the bed, forcing me and my mum right back. A porter smiled and thanked us and pushed the bed, complete with very ill-looking old lady, into the lift. A nurse accompanied them and made small talk with one of the visitors, asking about the weather outside and saying it might change.

I tried to hold my breath. Even after the bedridden patient had reached her floor and they wheeled her out, after the doors had closed, I kept my breathing as shallow as possible.

Finally, the doors opened for our floor and I very nearly ran out.

•

Gareth's mum was sitting by his bed. I always thought of her as a big, beefy woman with masses of curly blonde hair and quick-fire jokes. But as I walked into the Intensive Care Unit and saw her sitting there, with her hair tied back, bags under her eyes and her mouth turned down, I almost mistook her for someone else.

She looked up as we approached. For a moment, she seemed OK, then she was hugging my mum, tears spilling down her face.

Gareth had moved. They had shifted his bed to another part

of the room. It took a moment before the real shock hit me. No ventilator. There were plenty of monitors, but the ventilator was gone.

His mum finally noticed me. 'Kyle.' She wiped her eyes. 'It's good of you to come. You're a brave boy.'

I guess she knew about my incident when I last tried to see Gareth.

'Is he getting better?' I asked.

She looked at my mum and took a deep breath. 'They say he's stable. He's just in a deep, deep sleep.'

I wasn't stupid. I knew what a 'coma' was. Gareth even had a joke about one.

I tried not to think about that. It didn't seem right.

Without waiting to be invited, I stepped up next to Gareth's bed and took a look at my friend.

I could hear my mum behind me. 'Have they said anything more?'

Gareth's mum murmured, 'Not much. They seem to be a bit short on answers.'

I turned round. 'Do they know why he's in a coma?'

Gareth's mum gave a slight shake of her head. 'The policeman said something about the stuff you were burning in there. Maybe there was plastic or paint . . . something toxic. Some young doctor backed him up, talking all technical rubbish about chemicals and carbon monoxide, but the bottom line is they just don't know.'

I looked down at Gareth while our mums talked. A moment later, I got a tap on the shoulder. They were going for coffee. Would I be OK on my own for a bit?

Of course I would. Did they think I couldn't spend time

with my best friend just because he was like this? I was fine. Perfectly fine.

At least Gareth looked more like himself without that tube stuck to his face, without the hiss of a machine moving his chest.

'All right, man,' I said, shuffling up next to him. I checked to see that none of the nurses were too close, and then I got really annoyed at myself. I looked back down at my friend. 'Sorry. It's just weird with you lying there.'

No reaction. My mum was gone. Gareth's mum too.

I bit my lip, told myself I was doing OK. I had said something. I knew this was going to be tough and couldn't help thinking back to the time I sat next to my brother as he lay on his back in an incubator. This was different. If Gareth could hear me, then somewhere in his sleep, he would understand me. He would recognise my voice and know it was me. I wasn't here as a visitor; I was here to do a job. I was here to help fix my friend.

My eyes strayed to the repeating wave pattern on the monitors. Lines of various shape and colour streaming from right to left. The volume was turned right down, but I could still hear a faint *beep . . . beep . . . beep*.

It was almost in time with the gentle beat of music, quietly playing on the stereo next to his headboard. I recognised the track and couldn't help a smile.

'Simply Red?'

Gareth grinned. 'Who'd wake up to that?'

My mouth dropped, I blinked, but Gareth was just the same as before – eyes shut, face relaxed, breathing slow.

I kept my eyes on him, blinked a few times.

Gareth didn't move.

So I picked up the CD box that lay next to the stereo. 'I hope this is one of your mum's, and she didn't find it hidden in your room.'

His face never twitched.

Nothing.

'Well, I don't suppose she could sit here and listen to thrash metal.' Gareth's taste in music reflected his taste in horror stories. The more macabre, the better. 'Could you see these nurses trying to work with Slayer belting out.'

Gareth laughed and said, 'Yeah, *Angel of Death*.'

This time I definitely saw him grinning at me. He leaned to one side and quoted a handful of lyrics. 'Monarch to the kingdom of the dead!'

I whispered, 'Gareth?'

Gareth shook his head. 'She'd have a fit if she listened to half of the things that I do. Even so, there's no real excuse for Simply bloody Red.'

I glanced at the nurses' station. One of them looked over, gave me a smile of encouragement then went straight back to whatever form she was filling in.

Gareth rolled his eyes. 'Do us a favour, will you? Fetch me something decent.'

Again, I checked the nurses' station and looked back at Gareth.

Gareth smiled, then his face dropped. 'What?'

I closed my eyes tight. This wasn't happening.

When I opened them, Gareth was looking concerned. 'You OK, man?'

'You're in a coma, Gareth.'

Gareth smiled. 'You hear the one about the Indian waiter? Fell into a korma!'

'That's shit, Gareth.'

'You laughed at school.'

'It's hardly appropriate.'

'Bollocks, it's more suitable than ever. Gallows humour, Kyle.'

'You're not going to die!'

A hand touched my shoulder and I nearly jumped out of my skin.

The nurse by my side apologised. 'Didn't mean to startle you. It sounds like you're doing great.'

I snapped back to Gareth.

Still. Quietly breathing. Sleeping.

'Keep it up,' she said. 'If you need anything, just give me a shout.'

She walked away, and Gareth remained perfectly still.

•

When Gareth's mum returned, she looked a lot better.

'Thanks, Kyle,' she said, and she sounded genuine. 'It'll be good for Gareth to hear someone else chat to him.'

I just nodded and an awkward silence followed.

'You can come by and visit any time you like. The nurses understand.'

I looked again at my friend. 'I will. Thanks.'

And I was going to leave it there, but as I left I paused and turned. 'Could I bring him a few more CDs?'

•

Back in my bedroom, Gareth was standing next to the vivarium.

I wasn't looking at him. I was at my desk, a pencil in hand, scribbling furiously and definitely not looking behind. But I knew he was there, in his favourite place, looking at the scorpion.

'Good music,' he said.

I bit my lip. No point answering. No point at all. I kept drawing and listening to the CD playing in my little stereo. It wasn't something I'd normally put on.

'You bought it on the way home, did you?'

'I'm just checking it's OK.' I bit my lip again. I couldn't believe I'd spoken.

'Random choice, was it?'

I didn't answer.

'Do you know what that song's about?'

'No.' Except I did. I just didn't know it was on that particular album until I'd bought the thing.

It was my mum's idea. She'd heard what I'd said to Gareth's mum and as we came home, she said that if I wanted to buy a CD that he'd like, she would pay.

As we went into the music store, I had a good idea of what to look for. Gareth had been bringing stuff to my house for ages, desperately trying to convert me to bands like Morbid Angel and Napalm Death. I wasn't an expert, but I'd heard enough to know his mum was never going to sit listening to thrash- and death-metal. But Metallica were quite tame in comparison, so I picked out a CD and went to the counter.

Now that the song was playing on my stereo, I did recognise it.

Gareth let out a short laugh. 'It's about this bloke on a hospital bed . . .'

I gave in and turned round. 'You're not here.'

But he was. He was standing right by the vivarium, fully dressed, large as life.

He shrugged and tapped on the side of the vivarium. 'Harold. Harold? You want to come out?'

'No, it doesn't!'

'Are you going to pick him up again?'

'Like hell I am.'

'It was hardly his fault you got stung. You scared him.'

I couldn't believe this.

'That's because *you* scared *me*.' I was annoyed now and getting sick of whatever was making me *think* Gareth was in my room. I shut my eyes tight and pressed my thumbs so hard against my eyelids that it hurt. I sat like that for a good fifteen seconds, telling myself over and over, *he isn't here; he is not in my room; my best friend is in hospital and is not in my bedroom.*

I opened my eyes.

Gareth's face was full of concern. 'What's wrong?'

I rubbed my hands over my face, through my hair. 'I don't know.' I kept my eyes on the floor, refusing to look up. Finally, I had to ask, 'Why are you here, Gareth?'

'Why do you think?'

I wasn't prepared to play games. 'Just tell me.'

Gareth lowered his voice. 'It could have been you, Kyle. You could be the one stuck in this hospital bed. You could be the one who's going to die.'

'So what is this, some way of getting back at me?'

'No, man. The whole point is that Alex ran off. He *left* us there.'

I knew exactly what he was saying. It was the same thing

DS Miller had been hinting at, the same thing my mum had asked again and again in the hospital, the same thoughts I'd been struggling with myself.

I sat there in silence.

When I looked up, Gareth was still there. His attention was back on the vivarium. 'You can't let him beat you, Kyle. You can't let Alex win.'

He didn't look at me. Didn't need to. I knew exactly what he meant.

•

At eight o'clock the next morning, my mum was already up and about. When I stepped into the kitchen she was busy shortening the stems of flowers she'd picked from the garden. I dropped my school bag on the table and said, 'I think it's time I went back.'

She looked at me like I'd just told her I'd wet the bed. 'I thought we'd already discussed this.'

Yeah, but Gareth turned up, and we got talking . . .

'I have to go back at some point.'

'You also need time to rest. Another week or so isn't going to make much difference.' She had a nervous smile on her face, like she was trying to make light of the issue. 'I'm sure your teachers will understand. I'll write them a letter, I'll . . .'

'I've still got stuff to do. I'll fall behind if I don't.'

She paused. I knew she was thinking of a comeback.

'I'll ask your teachers for worksheets,' she said. 'You can catch up here.'

I put my hand on my school bag. 'I *need* to go back.'

She held my gaze for a moment, then relaxed.

'Well sit yourself down,' she said. 'The least I can do is make you a decent breakfast.'

ALEX

The rattle, creak and bang of the front door woke me up.

That would be my dad, leaving to get a paper.

Over the past few days I had become used to staying in bed until ten o'clock. I'd lie there and drift in and out of sleep or stare up at the ceiling until I felt I *had* to get up. It was a luxury my dad would never have allowed me before. But since I'd been in hospital he didn't seem to bother me about it. If I was up here, on my own, that meant I wasn't out there talking to people I shouldn't be.

But on that morning, when the door slammed shut, that thought was no longer any comfort. I didn't want to be left alone any more. Or maybe, I just didn't want to be doing anything my dad was happy with.

Suddenly, my room was more of a prison cell than a sanctuary and I knew that I wouldn't be able to take another day in this house.

I got out of bed and got ready. There was somewhere I needed to be. It would mean seeing Kyle again – seeing everyone – but it was something I had to do; not because I needed to get out of the house, but because I *wanted* to face the music. I had thought back again and again to that time in the cave, before it all went wrong, when it felt like we were mates – the three of us, Gareth too. It had felt like we were a gang – a small gang, yeah, but so what? It had felt good, and I wanted that back.

My mam nearly jumped out of her skin when I stepped into the kitchen.

'Alex. You're up early.' She had her right hand behind her, and as she took a step back I heard the unmistakable clink of a bottle against the radiator.

'It's not what it looks like,' she said, revealing the wine bottle that she'd been hiding from me.

The bottle was open. It couldn't have been from last night because my mam never, ever went to bed while there was still wine in the bottle.

'I wasn't drinking it,' she said. 'I was just looking, you know? You won't say anything to your dad, will you, pet?'

I think I felt more tired than angry, more sick of this endless spiral, of seeing this as her solution. I should have screamed at her, 'Call Joe. For Christ's sake, put the bottle down and call your big, gangster brother.'

I didn't want my dad beaten up, and I didn't want him killed. I just wanted him to stop belting my mam and turning her into this mindless zombie.

But I didn't scream, and I didn't shout. I just stepped past her to grab the milk from the fridge.

'I'm going to school.'

•

I went to the bus stop. There were about seven other kids there milling about in two groups. I caught them looking, and I heard their conversations dampen as I approached, but no one said a word to me directly. No one asked anything about the hospital or Kyle or Gareth and that suited me fine. By the time the bus came, they were back to their typical morning conversations about last night's TV or who fancied who.

From the moment I stepped on the bus I was aware of everyone's eyes on me, and I knew they were waiting for me to go upstairs so they could make some remark or other. So you know what I did? I sat downstairs, right at the front. I even twisted side on, so they knew for sure that I'd hear anything they had to say.

The bus pulled away, conversations started up, but no one mentioned my name.

KYLE

My mum had backed down on me going back to school, but she fussed over everything else. I put up with it, finished my toast, drained my glass and got up to go. She was at the door before me, grabbing her keys and jacket.

'I'll walk you to the stop.'

I was almost out of the door. 'What for?'

'Well, I'm going that way anyway.'

'You're rubbish at lying, Mum.'

'Fair cop. I just thought I'd see you on the bus. I'll stand right back, make it look like I'm off somewhere else.'

'I'll be fine.'

'Kyle? Just this once?'

It was one of those conversations I'd only win by it turning into a full-scale argument. If I was going back to school, I didn't want to start the day in a bad mood, or feeling guilty.

'You're not going to carry my bag, are you?'

She snorted. 'Fat chance.'

•

There were the same familiar faces at the bus stop. Just a few of them, all older than me. It was one of those moments when things hit home with renewed impact. Gareth was the only kid in my year to use this stop, and he probably wasn't going to be using it for a while.

If ever.

My mum broke my thoughts. 'You OK, pet?'

I thought fast. 'Just thinking about maths. What I'll have to catch up on.'

'Well don't. Your teachers know you've been in hospital and they know about Gareth. Promise me you'll take it easy.'

'I will.'

She kept staring at me.

'I *will*!'

We waited at the stop and made uncomfortable small talk – mostly my mum – about the morning being a little colder than yesterday. Just killing time really.

It was a relief when the bus turned the corner and began to slow down.

I didn't notice Alex until I boarded. I caught him looking at me, but only for an instant. As I passed, he kept his eyes down, he never said a word.

I kept going, finding a spare seat about three behind him.

When the bus pulled away, I looked out of the window to give my mum a wave.

But she wasn't looking at me.

It only took a second to realise who she *was* looking at. She was staring at Alex, and her eyes were wide.

I suppose she hadn't expected to see him going to school with me.

I felt a bit rotten, like I should get off the bus and tell her it was OK, that she had nothing to worry about. It wasn't like he was my best friend.

•

I don't think I ever want to be famous, not if it's anything like it was when I walked back into school. There were eleven hundred pupils in that school, and I hardly knew a third of them, but suddenly every single one of them knew all about me. Kids older than me, kids younger, kids I'd never even noticed before. They all knew me. I was the boy who survived. The boy whose best friend was in a coma.

But no one mobbed me. No one said anything while I was on the bus, no one rushed up to me when I stepped off, and even when I got to the spot where most of my classmates hung out, they didn't quiz me. Even so, I was aware of them *wanting* to ask stuff.

Alex didn't say a word either, but he was watching me from the far side of the yard. As my friends welcomed me back, but kept conversations safe, Alex stood on his own, just watching. I knew he wanted to ask stuff too. I could feel it.

He managed to hold off until lunch, when things were a little quieter.

I didn't see him at first. It was a look on Jamie's face, then another kid who was also with us. I turned round to see Alex walking towards us.

It was weird. He didn't say anything. He just sort of hovered until the others went away – each one getting the message without him even looking at them.

He watched them go, then looked at me. 'You made it back then.'

'Yeah.'

He looked about, checking the other boys were keeping their distance. 'It wasn't our fault you know.'

'What?'

'Gareth. What happened to Gareth. It wasn't our fault.'

'You made the fire.'

'And you told us to keep the ivy in place.'

I flushed with anger, 'We were only going to light a couple of candles. That would have been perfectly safe.'

'All I mean, Kyle, is that it was an accident. None of us knew what was going to happen. None of us knew we were in danger.'

'You did. You got out.'

'Kyle . . .'

The sound of the doors opening marked the end of dinner time and cut Alex short.

I took a final look at him before going inside. 'Just stay away from me, eh?'

•

He did as I asked and kept his distance for the rest of the day. Even so, it was a long day. The final bell came as a relief. I managed to get to the bus stop without any questions, and Alex didn't say a word. When he got on, he went upstairs, just like he'd always done, and I went to my regular seat downstairs.

When I got home I was greeted by the smell of my mum's cooking.

She was in the kitchen, and turned to give me a smile as I walked in.

'It's not quite ready,' she said, wiping her hands on a tea towel. 'I thought I'd do a lasagne. I know it's your favourite.'

I spotted the light on the deep fryer. 'With chips?'

'You can't have a lasagne without chips, can you?' She reached for the plates and casually asked, 'How was school?'

I shrugged. 'Nothing special.'

'What sort of things did you do?'

'You know – just school stuff.'

'You managed to get back into the flow OK?'

'Mum, I was fine. It was just a normal day.'

'Because if you don't think you're ready, you can still change your mind. It won't matter.'

'I can't really stay away when there's nothing wrong with me. Besides, Alex has gone back.'

Her face darkened. 'Well, that's a perfectly good reason for you to stay at home.'

'Why? What will that prove? The chances are he'll still be in my class next year.'

She snorted with disgust. 'Not if I can help it.'

'I don't sit next to him, if that's what you're worried about.'

'I would just rather you didn't have anything more to do with that boy.'

Oh, right. Like I was going to completely forget about Gareth and hospital and join the Alex Fan Club. I sighed in frustration. 'Why would I have anything to do with someone like Alex Crow?'

'You were in the cave with him, weren't you?'

'That was a one-off. We weren't exactly hanging out with him.'

'Oh, he just happened to turn up and start a fire?'

'He followed us. We didn't invite him. We didn't ask him to make a fire.'

Suddenly her voice was louder. 'So why didn't you just run away? There's no shame in that.' I could see she was squinting to fight back tears. 'There were two of you and only one of him. You could have both run away.'

'It wasn't like that. He was . . . he was trying to be friends.'

I had to look away because for a short time in that cave, it had been like we *were* friends. And with what he'd said at school – was he still trying? Why? After what had happened, why would he?

As I looked up, I saw her wipe her cheek with the back of a hand.

'I don't want you near that boy,' she sniffed. 'Kyle? I want you to promise. Promise me you'll keep away from him.'

'I'll try my best. I'll try to avoid him.'

But I didn't promise.

Later, when dinner was on the table, I kept replaying our earlier conversation. I was still annoyed that she had pretty much accused me of wanting to hang out with Alex. After everything.

She cut through my thoughts. 'You not hungry?'

I looked at my plate, realising I'd just been shifting the food about.

'I was thinking, that's all.'

She reached across and touched my hand. 'I'm sorry for

giving you a hard time earlier, Kyle. I didn't mean to get so angry.'

I almost nodded, but 'angry' wasn't the word. She'd been bordering on panic. What was so odd was it had come out of nowhere. I could have understood if she'd been like that at the hospital, straight after events, but not on my first day back at school. It was like she'd seen him this morning, sitting on the bus and . . .

I looked up. 'How did you know Alex?'

'Sorry?' She withdrew her hand.

'You recognised him,' I said. 'This morning, when I got on the bus. You were staring at him, and you *recognised* him.'

'Oh that.' She paused and looked down, fumbling for an answer. It was clear she was searching for a suitable lie. 'I saw him in the hospital, didn't I? I was just surprised he was back at school, like you.'

That didn't come close to working.

'No. It was different in the hospital, like you couldn't place him. But this morning, you looked like you knew him. You looked scared.'

Something about this was bugging me. I could see the pain in her face, like she was ready to give in, but instead she was holding back, choosing to stare at the wall rather than look at me directly.

I followed her line of sight and looked at the wall behind me.

A framed picture. A drawing. The drawing I'd done on my baby brother's first day of life.

'It's something to do with Christopher, isn't it?'

I couldn't see how, but from the way she looked from the picture to her plate, I knew I was right.

She just sat there, playing with her fork. I thought she would stay like that all night. But I was wrong, because without looking up, she started talking.

Nothing could have prepared me for what she said. No one could have told me how much it would hurt inside. No pain had ever cut so deep.

ALEX

I was on my bed, fully dressed, thinking of how I could get through to Kyle.

I could imagine my dad's reaction. 'You don't go begging and crawling to them. Let *them* come crawling to *you*.'

Which explained a hell of a lot about my dad. It also made me all the more determined to prove to myself I wasn't like him. What's so bad about admitting you've screwed up? Everyone does it once in a while.

But I'd tried, hadn't I? I tried talking to Kyle today and I'd got nowhere.

No!

That was my dad's attitude. A life soaked in failure. If at first you don't succeed, you shouldn't have bloody bothered.

It certainly wasn't me. I fought my battles and I won. So yeah, I'd tried, and I'd had a setback too. That didn't mean I should give up.

Like I said, no one's perfect.

The only thing close to perfection in this house was that drawing on my wall – Kyle's drawing.

It still looked amazing.

I hardly slept a wink that night. My mum's story was locked on constant replay inside my head and the only thought to break through was what I wanted to do to Alex.

But how? What could I ever do to someone like Alex Crow? I couldn't exactly walk into school with a baseball bat, could I? Not that I had one, but even if I did, Alex would probably get it off me before I got anywhere near him. People like me don't get even with people like him.

From the corner of the room, the scorpion shuffled about in its vivarium.

Stupid bloody thing.

I don't get you. He's so cool. I mean, a real, live genuine scorpion. It's big and black and terrifying. One sting from one of these can kill you.

Yeah, right. If its sting could kill, then maybe I would have a weapon worthy of Alex Crow. It might hurt like hell, but I had first-hand knowledge that it certainly wasn't fatal.

I lay on my bed thinking about this.

No, the scorpion's sting wasn't fatal.

But Alex didn't know that.

ALEX

When I woke up the next morning, I made a decision. I'd been mulling it over most of the night. It certainly wasn't easy, but in the end I decided to go for it.

I wanted to choose the right moment though, so when I got on the bus, I went back to my regular spot upstairs.

As the bus turned the corner at the bottom of the estate, I kept my eyes peeled for signs of Kyle.

And there he was.

I took a deep breath. I'd had cage fights that were easier than this.

When the bus stopped, I remained in my seat. Only when I saw Alex come downstairs and step off, did I get up.

I didn't want to wait until we were in school. I caught up before he reached the gates.

I called his name. 'Alex!'

He turned, not in the least surprised to see me.

'Kyle,' he said. He had a bag over his shoulder with a tube of rolled-up paper sticking out of the top. He let the bag slide off his shoulder, pulled the paper tube free and held it out.

But I wasn't going to be sidetracked. I had it all planned out in my head and needed to get right to the point. So I told him, 'I've got something for you.'

My hands were sweating as I unzipped my school bag. The biscuit tin was the only thing in there. The idea was to show him the tin, maybe give it a little shake just to rouse his curiosity, then get him to follow me – somewhere special.

But he stumped me by replying, 'Yeah, I've got something for you too,' and before I could get back on track, he pushed the rolled-up paper into my hand.

'It's yours,' he said.

'Mine?'

I hadn't planned for this. I dropped my bag and unrolled the paper.

I could hardly believe what I was seeing, and the first thing it brought to mind was Gareth.

Because Alex was right. It *was* mine. It was a copy of the cover of a CD that Gareth used to bring round. He'd begged me to draw it for him, saying, 'Go on, Kyle. You'll do a great job.' He even threatened to keep playing the CD until I gave in.

It took me three nights to complete, but Gareth was astounded. He was so happy, you'd have thought I'd just bought him a car. He said he was going to put it on his bedroom wall, but during our first week, when the art teacher asked for pictures to fill up the empty walls, Gareth gave it back and insisted I hand it in.

He was devastated when it went missing.

Seeing it again, holding it in my hands after so long . . . it was like a slap in the face.

Because it wasn't my picture at all.

This belonged to Gareth.

I looked up at Alex. 'You?'

He raised his eyebrows in a brief, silent apology. 'I've had it quite a while. I looked after it though, kept it safe.'

I couldn't get my head around this. 'You stole it?'

'It was nothing personal. I just liked the picture, you know?

I still think it's brilliant, but . . .' He took a deep breath. 'It's a way of saying sorry, Kyle. For everything. For chasing you, making the fire. Everything.'

The paper was shaking in my hands. I couldn't believe what I was hearing.

'Everything?'

'Yeah.'

I was so shocked by what he'd given me that I was hardly aware of him picking up my bag and saying, 'So what you got in there?'

'What?'

He was reaching inside, reaching for the tin. My hand flashed out and I snatched the bag back.

'Not here,' I said. 'Not with everyone looking.' I quickly zipped it up.

'Why not?'

'Because it's private, that's why.' I was aware of the other kids around us listening.

I leaned forward, my voice too quiet for prying ears, back to the lines I'd rehearsed all morning.

'It's something from Gareth. Something he'd like you to see.'

Alex looked confused. 'Gareth?'

'But not here.' I nodded towards the school fence, to the church spire that peeked over the trees behind. 'Up there.'

'The cemy?'

'Yeah. It's quiet. Private. You know?'

'What about school?'

I didn't answer. Instead, I started walking. After a few steps I turned and simply said, 'You coming or what?'

I was desperate for a drink. My mouth was so dry that I could hardly swallow, so as we passed a newsagent I told Alex to hang on. And he did.

I went inside and picked up a can of coke. As I did, something yellow on the knick-knack shelf caught my eye. I considered for a second, then nodded to myself and picked that up too. I paid for both and stepped back outside. Alex was still waiting.

'I never thought you'd be one to bunk off school.'

I didn't answer. I took a drink of coke. My hand was shaking and I had to hold the can tight to stop the pop from spilling. As we walked, I handed the can to Alex.

The cemetery was fairly modern – no ancient, leaning stones with eroded text and overgrown weeds threatening to hide them from the world. This place was large and well tended. The trees were evenly spaced. The grass was short, neat, and the marble headstones were clean and sharp. Many of the graves had fresh flowers on them.

It was beautiful. Just how it should be.

Alex strode slowly behind me.

'Is this far enough?' he asked. 'There's no one about.'

'Just a little further.'

Alex muttered something, but he followed, saying, 'Come on, Kyle. What's this all about?'

I reached into my pocket, and without a word I showed him what I'd bought.

'What's that? A toy?'

I changed direction again, this time crossing onto the grass, passing through the gravestones, walking between the plots. And then I came to a stop and waited for him to catch up.

'What's with the yellow car?'

I didn't answer. I was standing in front of a small plot. The soil was a curved mound – a sign that this was a fairly recent grave. The mound itself was tiny.

For a tiny coffin.

The head of the grave was marked by a simple wooden cross. On the cross, the engraved nameplate was the shape of a teddy bear. And there were several real teddy bears in among the flowers that surrounded the base of the cross.

'This is my brother,' I said.

Alex said nothing.

'His name's Christopher.'

'Yeah, I can read.' Alex's tone was slightly defensive.

'He doesn't have a proper headstone yet,' I said. 'He hasn't been here long enough.'

My mum had explained how the ground had to settle for at least six months. Christopher had been here for five. And that's how old he'd be now if he was still alive.

Alongside the teddies and flowers there were several small toys too. I leaned down and placed the car next to the tractor I'd brought last time.

'I come here sometimes to see him. He can't hear me, but I talk to him. He can't play with these toys, but I still buy them.'

'So why bring me here?'

I unzipped my bag, removed the tin and dumped the bag on the ground. I could feel Harold scrabbling about inside the tin.

Hey, you said it. You called him Harold. I really think you're making progress.

Alex asked the obvious question, 'What's in the tin?'

'Something for you.'

Don't do this, Kyle.

He wasn't here. Gareth was in bed, in hospital. And Alex was the reason why.

He'll kill him, Kyle. If Harold stings Alex, he'll fling him on the ground. He'll stamp on him. You might not care about Harold, but I do. He's a cool pet, man. Don't let Alex kill him.

I could hardly get my breath. My hands were shaking so much that the lid of the tin, which I'd already loosened, slipped off and landed on the grass.

'So what is it?' said Alex. He stepped forward to look into the tin.

Just tell him what you want to say. Just say it, Kyle. Don't use Harold.

It wasn't too late. I could chuck the thing in his face and run.

Alex stepped forward. 'What you got there?'

Just tell him, Kyle.

And then Alex was close enough to see.

'What the hell is that? Is that . . . is that a *scorpion*?'

I bent down, grabbed the lid and slammed it back on the tin.

'That's pretty freaky, Kyle. Why did you bring a scorpion to the cemy?'

And I screamed out, 'Because you killed him. That's why.'

'What?' His face screwed up like I was mad.

'Him.' I pointed to the grave. 'My brother. My mum recognised you, Alex. I said she'd made a mistake, but she insisted, saying she would never, ever forget the face of the boy who pushed past her that day.'

'What are you talking about?'

He had lost his defensive tone and seemed genuinely puzzled. If anything, that only made matters worse.

There was no going back now.

'Back in January,' I said. 'Right at the start of the year.' I even let out a short laugh. 'You probably won't even remember. You came running for a bus. There was only a small queue, just a few people. But you couldn't wait. You came running and jumped on the bus just as my mum was trying to step off. You knocked her flying. You even stopped to look back. You saw her lying in the road, but you went and sat down like it was nothing. Do you remember?'

Alex said nothing.

'She was pregnant. She was pregnant with my little brother. The bus driver came to help, but *you* . . . you were so pissed off at having to sit there and wait that you got back off the bus. I always thought it had just been an accident, but last night she told me the truth. And she told me it was you. You didn't even stop to apologise. And because of that, my little brother ended up here.'

Alex stared down at the grave.

I swallowed hard and picked up my bag.

'My brother is buried in that grave. My brother is dead.'

And Gareth is going to be next.

Those words stuck in my throat. No. No, that wasn't going to happen.

Because you put him in a coma.

You lit the fire.

It was an accident. None of us knew what was going to happen. None of us knew . . .

I clenched my fists and eyes. *Shut up!*

And then I looked directly at Alex and I said what I needed to say.

'You killed him, Alex. You killed my baby brother.'

It was out. I'd gone as far as I could and I was ready for whatever Alex was going to throw back at me. Let him kick, punch, do whatever he liked. It couldn't hurt any more than this.

I stood waiting. Ready.

But Alex didn't fight. He didn't argue. He just looked at me and then down at the grave. He actually seemed to shrink.

Good.

ALEX

Kyle left me standing by the grave.

Had that really been a scorpion in his tin? A live one? Had he been expecting me to put my hand in there? Jesus.

Below me, by my feet, the small car stood next to the other toys on the grave.

I could remember the incident Kyle had been talking about. It was the day after my dad killed Jim Banks. The day I decided to get it over and done with. I'd run for the bus and as soon as the doors opened I pushed my way in, knocking some woman aside in the process. She fell over, but I didn't really care. All I was thinking about was the mess I was in. If I sat down, the bus would move and I could finish it. I could still see images of the blood on the floor, ringing out the mop, the swirl of red in that filthy old sink. Right at that moment, I hadn't cared what happened to me, I just wanted my dad to pay for what he'd put me through.

But the bus didn't move. The driver was outside next to that woman, while inside, people were tutting and moaning about being late while I was lost in a world of what would happen if I stayed on the bus, if I followed through with my plan.

So that woman lying on the ground, I guess she'd saved me, and as I'd left the bus, I couldn't help letting out a small laugh because I had come so close – so *painfully* close – not only to grassing up my own dad, but grassing up pretty much everyone who'd been in the warehouse that night, including Joe and a whole load of real, hardcore villains.

They'd have taken me apart.

But now, standing by the grave, I saw the other side of the coin.

My brother is buried in that grave, and you're the one who put him there.

I'd done this?

You killed him, Alex. You killed my baby brother.

See his fatha's eyes.

No.

No!

I wasn't like him. My dad was a joke. Small and thin, stuffed into his armchair, scratching away at a crossword, angry and paranoid, irritated at everything around him, taking it out on my mam.

And that's when it finally hit home.

How long would it be until I was standing by *her* grave, wishing I'd done something, said something? If my dad could lose his rag and kill Jim Banks, it was only a matter of time before he did the same to my mam.

I couldn't go to the police. I knew that. But there was one person I *could* go to. Someone I should have spoken to a long, long time ago.

Joe.

KYLE

The envelope was standing up against the gravestone. It had been placed at an angle, its lower corner damp and crumpled where it touched the soil. The envelope had a single word –

CHRISTOPHER

My mum frowned and picked it up. 'What's this?'

I got a bad feeling. I wanted to tell her not to read it, to snatch it from her, tear it up and throw it away, but it was already open and she was taking out the card.

'What is it?' I asked.

All I could see was the front of the card – a simple design with cut-out flowers.

My mum shook her head and put the card in her bag.

'Nothing.'

I wanted to ask the obvious, but I already knew the answer.

My mum tidied the grave, pulling up any shoots of weeds, replacing last week's flowers with the ones she'd bought today. She noticed the toy car I'd placed the other day and smiled, but she didn't say anything other than, 'Looks nice,' when she stood back to take it all in.

She put an arm around me. 'You want to stay for a while?'

'No, I'm OK.'

And I was.

ALEX

I didn't hang about. I wanted to see Joe as soon as possible, and the easiest place to track him down was the warehouse. So on Friday evening I left the house alone. I had planned to get there early and have a word with Joe before the place filled up, but I didn't count on just how long it would take to get there.

As I approached, I could hear the muffled boom, boom, boom of music coming from within. Things were under way and the door was closed.

I took a deep breath and turned the handle.

The bouncer was just inside the door.

'Hello, stranger,' he said with a grin. 'Didn't know you were fighting tonight.'

'Joe wants to see me,' I said.

'Over by the bar.'

Easy as that. I was in.

Joe spotted me as I walked over.

'Alex, good to see you again.' He hitched up his belt and appeared to grow in height. 'Normally, we don't let young spectators through the door, but I'll make an exception for you.'

This took me by surprise, and all I could say was, 'Thanks.'

'So what's with the visit? Just curiosity, or are you thinking of coming back?' He tipped his head towards the cage. 'A lot of water has passed under the bridge since you were last here.' His tone was friendly, but I knew exactly what he was meaning. Of course I did. It was precisely what I'd come here to talk about. But rather than talk, I found myself drawn back towards the cage.

It stood there, just as ugly as ever, and I felt something inside me jump. The whole scene was hypnotic. The same sickly, stale smell, the same punters, even the same old rock music.

'What's the matter?' asked Joe. 'You want to step inside?' He looked at the bloke next to him and laughed. 'We've seen the exact same thing with boxers, haven't we? They decide to pack it in, then they turn up at a match. Once they see the ring, that's it.'

He knew exactly what to say. It took an enormous effort not to look at the cage. I had to remind myself why I was here.

'It's a sad day when a promising young fighter gives it up,' said Joe.

I could feel a lecture coming on, so I quickly cut in, 'Who's fighting tonight?'

Joe nodded to the bloke next to him. 'That's the expression I was talking about. He wants to get back in, doesn't he?'

The other agreed. 'It never leaves you.'

And they were right. I could feel the thing pulling me like a magnet.

I repeated, 'Who's fighting?'

'I am.'

The voice came from behind, and I knew before I turned, that it was Neil.

It was the first time I'd seen him since his birthday. He was back in his familiar get-up. No poncy boxer's robe, nothing flash, just a sleeveless New Model Army T-shirt and a pair of knee-length shorts. The only changes were the tattoos – a pair of swallows either side of his throat and the Sunderland AFC 'Black Cats' logo on his arm. I guess turning seventeen came with badges.

He held a bottle of water in his right hand, took a swig and said, 'Haven't seen you for a long time, Alex. Couldn't hack it, eh?' he shook his head in disgust.

'Pack it in, Neil,' said Joe.

Neil reached out a long arm – deliberately slow – going for my face, either to slap my cheek or for some other way of riling me.

I smacked his hand away. Neil just laughed and took another drink from his bottle.

'How are you feeling?' asked Joe. 'I heard you had a bad chest.'

'I'm fine.'

'Well you know me, Alex. I'd love to see you back, but there's no juniors fighting tonight.'

'What about Neil?'

Neil pretended to choke on his drink. 'As if.'

Even Joe smiled, 'Neil's not a junior any more. This is his

second adult fight tonight.' He looked at his son. 'You ready?'

'Raring to go.' Neil looked over at the cage. His opponent was limbering up by the side. He was as tall as Neil, dark skinned and muscular. Neil didn't seem phased at all. 'Watch and learn, Alex.' He gave me a hard slap on the shoulder and turned away, walking towards the cage.

I looked through the crowd, searching for my dad, thinking back to the reason I'd come here and the things I wanted to say. I just didn't know how to start.

A cheer came from the crowd and I looked up. The MC was in the cage welcoming everyone and going over the evening's events. There was no point in dragging this out. I was more scared of losing my bottle than saying what I had to say, so in the end I took a breath and decided to go for it.

'Joe? I think there's something I need to tell you.'

But at the same time, Neil's name was announced. Joe yelled a cheer and clapped his hands. Neil and his opponent had entered the cage.

'Uncle Joe?'

He leaned down, but didn't take his eyes off Neil. 'What is it, Alex?'

'I need to tell you something. It's important.'

'It's what?' Suddenly he roared out, 'GO ON, SON,' and was met by cheers from those around him. He put a hand on the back of my neck. 'If it's about coming back, don't worry. We'll talk about it after the fight, eh? When things calm down a little. Go and get yourself down the front; cheer your cousin on.'

I couldn't believe I was being knocked back, but there was no point trying to talk with a fight under way. So I did like

Joe said. I went down to the front and tried to think of how I was going to tell him.

•

Neil's opponent looked terrifying. He must have been a serious bodybuilder or something; he was built like a tank. But Neil made the first move – he shot forward and the two fighters locked arms. Neil struggled, his muscles knotted, and I could see the strain in his face. I could also see that he was losing the battle.

People around me were shouting, 'Keep at him, Neil,' and 'Don't let up.'

But his opponent was forcing him down. When Neil dropped to his knees a cheer rang out from the far side of the room, a groan from this side followed by a resounding, 'Oooohh,' as the other lad released and knocked Neil flying with a right hook.

That's when I saw my dad, a bottle of lager in one hand – no doubt a betting slip in the other – and the hint of a smirk on his face. For a moment I thought I'd just imagined it, but when Neil was knocked down a second time, that smirk was definite, and I watched in growing anger as he took a single drink from his bottle. With that simple movement, my suspicions were confirmed and I whispered, 'Bastard.'

With a crash, one of the fighters smashed against the side of the cage, causing me to jump back. It was Neil. He rebounded off the bars and hit the floor. The other fighter prepared to body slam.

I forgot my dad and for a moment it was me in that cage. I could feel the canvas beneath me, knowing instinctively which way to roll, how to flip up onto my feet and take the initiative.

I screamed out, 'Move. Move!'

And Neil rolled, just as I would have done, and made his escape just in time. The other fighter slammed onto empty canvas while Neil managed to twist onto his knees and catch the other fighter by surprise.

The crowd on Joe's side of the room went wild. Neil was on his opponent's back, locked one arm under his neck and forced his knee into the middle of his spine. At the same time, he grabbed his own wrist and pulled his arm tight across the other's throat. It was one of the most painful holds Carlos had taught us and Neil had executed it perfectly.

I was screaming through the mesh, 'Go on, Neil. You've got him. Hold him there! Hold him!'

With his teeth bared yellow, his face dripping blood and sweat, Neil pulled the hold tighter. His opponent struggled, kicked, twisted, but in the end, he had no choice. His free hand reached out . . .

Slap . . . slap . . . slap . . .

The audience went wild. All around me people were on their feet. Supporters of the other guy were clapping too – showing respect to a superb win.

Only my dad looked pissed off. He spat on the floor and headed back towards the bar.

I made my way around the cage, through the tables and chairs and stepped up behind him. 'Not collecting your winnings?'

He glanced over his shoulder. He didn't look at my face, just my feet, then turned away.

'Chucked in seventy quid,' he grumbled. 'Wouldn't have won much back anyway, the odds were shit.'

'You bet on the other lad, didn't you?'

He spat a bit of chewed fingernail out of his teeth. 'What did you expect? A fucking dead cert – so they said.'

I couldn't hide my disgust. 'Would you bet against me if I was in there?'

This time he did look at me, then he sneered and took a drink.

And like that . . . it all made sense. I actually felt sick realising how blind, how stupid I'd been.

'You did, didn't you? That night. You bet against me.'

He knew exactly what I was talking about, but tried to make out otherwise. 'What night?'

'You put down three hundred quid,' I said. 'You'd never have put that much if there was a risk. The lower the odds, the more you need to put down – you told me that yourself. That's why you risked so much money. You were convinced I'd lose.'

'What the hell are you talking about, boy?'

'I'm talking about the night you murdered Jim Banks.'

He eyes locked on mine. Oh, I had his attention now.

'You want me to say it again?' I said. 'A little louder?'

His eyes flashed, but I saw fear, not fury. 'Don't you dare.'

The music was loud. But that wouldn't stop anyone close by overhearing us.

He stepped forward. 'Don't even joke about that. You understand?'

And suddenly, Joe was next to us, his voice as jovial as ever. 'Great fight, eh. What do you think, Will? Neil did pretty damn good.' He was beaming with pride. 'You see all the action, Alex?'

It was too late to let things drop. It was now or never. So I kept my eyes on my dad, and spoke loud and clear. 'My dad's got something he wants to tell you.'

His eyes were burning now. Terror, fury, disbelief. I thought he was going to swing for me, right there in front of Joe. Instead he hissed, 'One more word, boy, and it'll be the last thing you'll ever do.'

Joe was looking from my dad to me. 'Word about what?'

But my dad didn't stick about. 'I'll see *you* at home.' He dumped his bottle on the bar and pushed past me.

Joe looked confused. 'What was all that about?' Then he shouted after my dad, 'Will? WILL!'

But my dad was out the door. He didn't look back. To him, that was the end to it, like he knew I wouldn't overstep the line. That cocky confidence that he could leave me with a threat and walk out, slam his car door and head for home.

'Alex,' said Joe. 'Is everything all right, son?'

I bit the sides of my thumb. Around me, people were passing by, going to the bar, talking about the fight, laughing, chatting. My dad was driving home in his foulest mood yet.

Joe moved closer, put a hand on my back. 'You want to tell me?'

And out of nowhere, my hands were shaking. In a low voice – it didn't even sound like my own – I said, 'It was him.'

Joe's brow creased. 'It was him, what?'

'My dad. He killed Jim Banks.'

There. It was out. Nothing could bring it back now.

Joe said nothing, so I added, 'You were right. I did see

255

something. I was there when Jim was in the bogs. And I was there when my dad came in and sent me out. My dad came out. Jim didn't.'

Joe moved me away from the bar. 'I hope you realise what you're saying, Alex. Are you sure about this?'

I shook my head, hardly able to believe what I was saying. 'I saw the knife in his pocket. There was blood. He told me to shut up, and the next thing I know, I'm in there cleaning up the mess.'

Joe's expression was serious, angry, yet I could see him nodding as he thought it through.

'He lost a big bet that night,' I said, 'and he blamed Jim for it.'

Joe's expression gave nothing away. 'So why say something now?'

I looked down, but Joe wouldn't allow me thinking time and shook my shoulder hard. 'Hey! Why now?'

And from nowhere I shouted, 'Because I'm sick of him taking it out on my mam!'

If telling him about Jim Banks didn't knock the wind out of Joe, then this certainly did. He seemed to deflate a little, so I kept going before I lost the nerve.

'Every other day,' I said, 'at the slightest thing, he goes off on one. He beats the living shit out of her. She's terrified, too scared even to tell Aunty Pat.'

Joe was breathing through his nose, slowly, loudly. Then he nodded quietly to himself, gave my shoulder a squeeze and let go. 'Good lad, Alex.'

•

Joe shouted to a bloke nearby, told him he had to go out for a while, might not make it back, then he told me to go outside and wait by his car. I did so without question. Five minutes later, he came out with some other bloke in tow – tall, with a flat-top and wide shoulders.

'This is Len,' said Joe. 'He's an old friend. Knows your dad too.'

Len hardly glanced at me. He went directly to his own car, already briefed that he had to follow. I got in the passenger seat of Joe's Jag.

'You think he'll have gone home?' asked Joe.

'If he's as angry as I think he is . . . then yeah.'

I didn't want to spell it out what he'd be doing.

Joe sat back, with so much leg room that his fat arms were almost straight, and pulled out of the car park. He drove with unnerving calm and silence. I had to bite my lip, physically stopping myself from telling Joe to put his foot down. All I could think of was my dad, already home, and what he'd be doing – shouting, hitting the walls, looking for the slightest excuse for an argument, a reaction, then . . .

I looked out of the window, trying to find things to occupy my mind. Groups of men going from bar to bar, laughing, shouting, singing and enjoying their Friday night out. Packs of young women, barely dressed, some with bottles or burgers in their hands, laughing and jeering at each other.

The car's radio was on, but barely audible. I found myself straining to hear the music, adverts, traffic reports, doing anything and everything to avoid worrying about what I'd done, and what Joe was *going* to do.

Eventually I could see the Penshaw monument, lit up,

illuminated yellow against the darkening blue sky. We passed, then turned in through the houses, into my road, and came to a quiet halt outside my house. My dad's car was in the drive.

'Alex, I want you to stay here.'

I nodded and watched Joe get out. Len parked behind us and followed Joe to the front door. They didn't bother to knock; Joe just turned the handle and walked in.

I sat in silence. From nearby, maybe a street away, I heard a car wheel-spin and pull away. Down the bottom of our road, some woman was shouting for her kids, telling them it was time to come in. In my own house, the curtains were drawn, but there was nothing to see.

What was going on in there? Was Joe telling my dad what I'd said? Was my dad talking him round, calling it a stupid childish prank, a way of getting him back for betting against me. I could imagine Joe and Len walking back out of the house, saying, 'Sorry for the trouble, Will,' and hauling me out of the Jag, telling me to get in the house and not to make up any more bloody stories.

The front door opened.

But it wasn't Joe that came out. It was my mam. She had a handkerchief pressed up to her face. She was crying and Len was right behind her

I opened the car door and got out. That's when I noticed the side of her face.

'Mam?'

'It's OK, Alex,' said Len. 'Looks like we got here in the nick of time.' He stepped forward, lifted the latch on the passenger seat. 'Jump in the back.'

'Why? Where are we going? Where's Joe?'

'Don't worry. Joe's having a word with your dad.

'Where are we going?' I asked again.

'Joe told me to take the two of you to his house, drop you off with your aunty Pat. Then I'm coming back to help out.'

'Help out? What do you mean? Help out with what?'

'It's not for me to say, son.' He got in the driver's side, adjusted the seat, then turned and said, 'One more thing. Joe said to keep quiet about all of this. You understand me?' His eyes flicked towards my mam and I knew exactly what he was saying. She hadn't been told what my dad had done.

'I understand.'

KYLE

Next morning, we went to the hospital.

Gareth's mum was there, just like before, but this time she seemed a lot brighter. She came straight over, hugged my mum and gave me a big smile.

'Thanks for coming back, Kyle. I told Gareth you'd be visiting.'

There was music playing on the stereo. Pop music.

'I brought him a CD,' I said.

'He'll like that.'

My mum handed me her bag. 'Go on, put it on for him.'

As I stepped up to the bed, she asked Gareth's mum if there was any news.

The response was quite positive. 'There's been some brain activity. The doctor said that's a good thing.'

I dumped my mum's bag by the stereo and looked for the CD.

The envelope we'd found on Christopher's grave was still in there, right next to it. The contents were still a mystery. I'd tried asking about it last night, but my mum avoided the question. I could have waited until she was settled in front of the TV and hunted for it, but I had never gone through her bag before and didn't want to start now.

But this was different. She'd given me her bag. It was open, and there was the envelope, just looking up at me.

I glanced over my shoulder. They were talking, occasionally looking at the bed.

I slipped the envelope out and looked at the card inside.

Just as I finished reading, I heard my mum call, 'Kyle?'

I've been caught, I've been caught.

As quickly as I could, I slipped the card back inside its envelope, and back in the bag. 'Yes?'

'Not too loud, eh? And pass my bag over. We're going to head off for a cuppa, give you a bit of time together.'

Trying to sound relaxed when you're almost shaking is tough. 'Yeah.' I handed her the bag. 'Here you go.'

I put the CD into the stereo and watched them leave.

Gareth lay on the bed breathing quietly.

Why had Alex written that card?

Was if for my mum, or for me?

Was this his way of trying to make up? Still? After he'd done this to Gareth?

And what if it hadn't happened? What if the fire hadn't been so big? Would the three of us be friends? Or would it be Gareth and Alex, best mates, telling stories, hanging out.

Well that couldn't happen now, could it?

I had to bite my lip to keep these thoughts at bay. What

was I thinking? That Gareth was better off in a coma? What kind of friend was I to be glad of something like this?

Of course I wasn't glad. I was just . . . angry. I wished I'd never read that bloody card. I wished Alex had never bothered.

I grabbed Gareth's hand. 'You're going to be OK.' I squeezed hard. 'You're going to wake up, and when you do we're going to come up with more stories than ever. Even me. I'll come up with them too. Really scary ones.'

Gareth lay there, perfectly relaxed while I wracked my brain for something suitable.

'Like, one about a kid who buys a pet scorpion,' I said. 'And he thinks it's just a normal one, like Harold, but it isn't. It's . . .' I stumbled. I was rubbish at this. What would Gareth say? 'It was from Africa or somewhere.' God, that sounded rubbish, but I felt a slight squeeze on my hand so I pushed on. 'Yeah. It was from Africa, and although it looked black, it was more of a deep brown, and its sting *was* lethal.'

There was a sudden change to Gareth's breathing – a slightly deeper breath.

I was doing OK. 'So it could kill. It could kill you in seconds. But on the day this kid found that out, he was so shocked that he bumped into the vivarium. It tipped over and the scorpion escaped.'

I stopped, suddenly realising what had happened.

He'd squeezed my hand! At the start of my story, Gareth had squeezed my fingers.

He took another, deeper breath.

'Nurse?'

And then his breathing relaxed, so I gripped his hand tight.

My voice was shaking. 'The problem was, the boy was standing in bare feet, and he knew the scorpion was somewhere on the floor.'

Nothing.

'And the floor was a complete mess. That thing could be anywhere.'

Another deep breath and a definite, *definite* squeeze on my fingers.

I was aware of the nurse at the bed, but I pushed on. 'And he was the only one in the house, so he couldn't just stand there. He lifted a foot and . . .'

My mouth went dry.

'Gareth?'

ALEX

When Uncle Joe came back to the house, all he said was that my dad had left and he wouldn't be bothering me or my mam again.

Aunty Pat wasn't satisfied. She was sitting at the kitchen table, the first-aid box still open in front of her, my mam sitting to her left.

'And what if he does?' she demanded.

Joe just looked tired. 'He won't.'

'You're sure about that?'

My mam didn't even look up. She just sat, staring at the cup in front of her – nothing stronger than sweet tea.

Joe sighed. 'He's gone, Pat. Forever.'

'And if he does come back?'

'What do you want me to do, go back and change the locks?'

'It would be a damn good start. I don't want Meg leaving this house until I know for certain that bastard can't get anywhere near her. Look at her *face*, Joe. Look at what he did to her.'

Joe rubbed a hand across his chin. 'Don't worry. It's next on the list. First thing in the morning, I'll go round and I'll get it all sorted out.'

•

I made sure I was up the next morning, I didn't give Joe a choice. I was going with him.

Joe didn't argue. He just shrugged and said, 'Fair enough.'

He made himself a sandwich and sat down.

'He won't be there,' he said. 'Just in case that's what you're expecting.'

'Why?' I asked. 'What did you do?'

'It doesn't matter, Alex. He's gone.'

'What's wrong? You don't think I'm old enough to know. You think it's too much for a kid like me?'

Joe looked at me for several long seconds.

He grabbed his sandwich, took another bite and got up. 'In the car.'

•

Joe was right. My dad wasn't there. He'd taken our car and gone, but he'd left one hell of a mess.

The front door was open when we got there, and for a moment I thought we'd been burgled. As I walked into the hallway and saw the things scrawled on the walls, I knew we hadn't.

My dad had used paint. He must have used every single pot he hoarded in the shed, and he'd slung the lot over the walls and windows, taking time to write 'BITCH' in giant letters, right in the hallway. There were other, similar, messages throughout the house. But that was only part of it.

Windows had been smashed, holes punched in the walls, shelves ripped down. The TV was gone – but the stereo was in bits. He'd taken a sledgehammer to the kitchen. Upstairs, he must have used that same sledgehammer to crack holes in the bath. The sink and toilet were smashed.

My bed was in one piece, but in their bedroom, the mattress was soaked with paint and the wooden frame of the bed splintered and broken. He'd done the wardrobe too. The doors were ripped off, the mirrors smashed, and strewn about the bedroom and the upstairs landing were the remains of my mam's clothes. Everything had either been torn, splattered with paint or cut up.

Joe didn't look particularly shaken. He was angry, but he didn't seem shocked.

'Collect anything you want, Alex. You can't bring your mam back here.'

•

Joe didn't dwell on details when he told my mam and Aunty Pat, he just gave them the basic facts – my dad had made a mess; he'd caused a lot of damage and ripped up some clothes. He didn't tell her about the graffiti messages or any specifics. In fact, he changed tone as soon as Aunty Pat said, 'Well let's hope that means he's gone for good.'

'The place will be as good as new in no time,' said Joe. 'Better than new. I've got a few lads in there right now. And hey . . .' He touched my mam's chin to get her to look up. 'You can thank young Alex for that. He's a star. As soon as I mentioned his name, those lads offered to do the work for bottom whack. I'll cover the rest.'

My mam looked grey. 'How much are you talking about?'

'What? I can't do a good deed for my little sister? Don't worry about it. All you need to think about is moving on, yeah?'

She let her eyes drop, so Joe bent down and repeated, 'Yeah?'

She gave a reluctant nod, even managed a small smile.

'That's more like it,' said Joe. He stood up, clamped a hand on my shoulder and said, 'You've got a good lad here, Meg. He's got guts, and a good head on his shoulders. He'll see you all right, won't you, Alex? You'll look after your mother for me.'

She managed another smile, and for the first time that day, I think I managed one too.

Joe kept going, 'He's a good boy this one. Going to be a big name one day.' And he looked right at me. 'I'm serious, Alex. We all told you last night. You could be good. Really good. I'm talking World Class.' He lowered his voice slightly. 'There's a lot of money to be made out of this, Alex. Big money. *Legal* money, if you take the risk.'

This threw me a little and I couldn't help a frown.

Joe smiled. 'Things are changing, Alex. This "Ultimate Fighting", as our Neil calls it, is massive in the States. TV audience. Sponsorship. Sometime soon, it'll be the same here. All above board, all legal. It just needs the right people.'

I was almost taken along with it. But then something my dad said came back to me.

Joe only cares about Joe.

I shook my head.

'Hey. Look around. How do you think I got myself a lovely big house like this? No one gave me those nightclubs. It's all about risk, Alex. And you know all about risk, don't you? You took one hell of a risk. You stood up for your mother and you did the right thing. If it wasn't for you, she'd be in hospital right now.' He turned to face my mam, his hand remaining firmly on my shoulder. 'He's a good kid. He knows how to make things right, when to speak up. And that takes guts.'

But I dropped my eyes and I just muttered, 'Yeah,' because my dad's words had put doubt in my mind, and that had got me thinking about other things . . .

. . . like the card I'd left on that grave.

I wasn't that brave, was I?

KYLE

I was in the front room when the doorbell rang. I got up to answer it, but my mum was already there. When she saw Alex, her face turned to stone.

Alex shifted back half a step. 'You got the card.'

It wasn't a question, and he didn't wait for much of a reaction before biting his bottom lip then asking, 'Can I come in?'

My mum paused. I was ready to run forward and slam the door at her request, but to my surprise, she said, 'Yes.'

She led him into the front room and sat down. She sat on the edge of an armchair, her back straight, no expression on her face. Alex sat on the sofa opposite looking decidedly uncomfortable.

'Well?' she said.

Alex looked up, but only briefly.

'Kyle told me about the baby,' he said. 'He showed me the grave.'

My mum shot a look at me. 'You told him?'

'Yeah.' I should have felt proud about it, but her look made me feel guilty, like I had to explain myself. I blurted out, 'I *had* to tell him. Tell him what he'd done. He didn't have a clue.'

Her eyes dropped, her expression sad, disappointed. She looked back at Alex. 'So when Kyle told you about Christopher, you decided to write the card?'

Alex nodded. 'Yeah.' He paused for a moment. 'I never knew you were pregnant. Honestly. I didn't even notice.' He paused again. 'I had a few things on my mind that day.'

My mum said nothing, but I felt like taking over this conversation and shouting, *Oh, really? Things on your mind? What's so important that you don't notice knocking a pregnant woman off her feet?*

If I was older, stronger, I'd have grabbed him and thrown him out of the house.

Alex looked down at his hands, at the carpet and I could feel myself getting more and more angry. He shouldn't even *be* here.

And then he looked up.

'My dad . . .' he sniffed, shook his head slightly, wiped his nose with the back of his hand. 'He . . .'

Alex trailed off.

My mum sat back a touch. 'He what?'

Alex looked up, his eyes firmly on my mum.

He took a deep breath.

ALEX

So I said, 'He used to hit my mam.'

I left it hanging. It wasn't what I wanted to say, but it certainly cut them short.

Kyle didn't say a word. He didn't come up with any remarks or challenge me, and neither did his mam. It was suddenly very quiet. Deathly quiet. No clock to tick. No sounds from outside. Nothing.

I decided to start at the beginning.

'I've got an uncle. He runs a few nightclubs. He's got a boxing club too. And upstairs they do a different kind of fighting . . .'

Kyle's mum was shocked when I explained.

'Cage fighting?'

I didn't want this to cloud things. 'It's not as bad as it sounds. A bit like kick-boxing.'

I told them about the warehouse and the kind of people

that went there, about my dad putting bigger and bigger bets. And the night when it all went wrong.

But I didn't mention Jim Banks, and I didn't mention the murder.

I wanted to, you know? That's how I planned to start this whole thing; that's what I was supposed to be building up to.

But it didn't happen. It didn't feel right. When Kyle's mum reacted the way she did just to the idea of cage fights, I knew it would have been too much. She'd be dumped with a whole lot of worry about whether or not to report the whole thing. Because that's what decent people do, don't they? Decent people stay on the bus and go to the police. Decent people don't have an Uncle Joe.

So I cut the story short, and I changed things about a bit. I told them about the fight I should have lost, and the chaos in the crowd, and I told them about my dad betting on my opponent, and going off it when he lost all that money.

'He was furious,' I said. 'But he ended up taking it out on my mam. He beat the hell out of her.'

And yeah, it was a lie, but really it was just the timing that was out. When I said those words, instead of the blood in the toilet, I was picturing my mam's face when Len brought her towards the car.

So I kept going.

'I wandered around the next day trying to think what to do. That's when I saw the bus. I decided, there and then, to go to the police. I didn't want to dwell on it, or I'd lose my bottle, so I ran as fast as I could and pushed my way through the doors. I was so messed up, I hardly noticed you. I definitely didn't realise you were pregnant. I found a seat and tried to switch off. But then I got scared. Like I said, some of the people that watched the fights were pretty scary. Not the sort of people you'd want after you. I thought that if I said something to the police they'd ask questions about what caused my dad to be so angry and they'd find out about my uncle and the warehouse and it would all come back to me.'

I looked up.

'So I got up. I saw you lying there, and all I could think was that you'd damn near saved my life. But I still never realised you were pregnant. I just wanted to get out of there.'

There was a pause, then Kyle's mum's said, 'So you didn't go to the police?'

For a moment, I wasn't sure what to say. I shrugged. 'It's sorted out now. My dad's gone. For good.'

I meant to rub my face, my eyes, but I noticed how much my hand was shaking and paused.

That's when she leaned forward and her hand touched my knee.

KYLE

She said, 'Thank you.'

I was shocked. I thought she'd have gone wild, but she didn't, and when I looked at her, despite the tears in her eyes, she was smiling.

'And thank you for the card,' she added.

Alex just nodded. 'I wanted to do something. But then Joe said some stuff about doing the right thing, and it hit home that a note on a card wasn't enough.' He paused. 'So here I am. I'm sorry for everything that happened. I'm sorry I made a fire too big and what happened to Gareth and . . .'

My mum put a hand on his. 'Shh. It's OK.'

Alex got up and wiped his eyes. 'I'd better go.'

'No. Stay.'

Alex was on his feet, shaking his head.

My mum got up too. 'Alex?' She moved so he couldn't avoid her eyes. 'It was a brave thing to come here and say these things. I'm not sure I could have done that.'

Again, he shook his head and made to walk past her, but she moved a hand, gently stopping him. 'Really, Alex. There's not many people who'd go out of their way to explain things like this.'

Alex paused. 'I did it for both of you. Kyle too.' He turned and looked at me. 'I didn't want you thinking I was just a psycho, you know? Other people might think that; I really don't care.'

I felt a bit uncomfortable. 'What makes me any different?'

Alex smiled and shook his head like I was asking the stupidest question ever. 'Because you're a shit-hot artist, man. I'm not so bad at times, but you . . . you're in another league.'

My mum looked at the two of us and gave a long, deep sigh. 'I think you two could do with a bit of time on your own, eh?'

Alex looked like he didn't quite believe her. 'It's OK for me to stay?'

'Did Kyle ever tell you he designed a backdrop for a rock band? It's true. He's got a photo on his wall, haven't you, Kyle?'

I tried to shrug it off like it was nothing.

Then she added, 'He's got a pet scorpion up there too.'

Alex looked at me. 'Was that thing real?'

I couldn't help a small grin. 'It's upstairs.'

•

Up in my room, Alex seemed more interested in the drawings pinned here and there than he did the vivarium.

275

He wasn't just looking at my pictures, he was examining them up close, then standing back saying, 'Amazing,' and 'Stunning, just stunning.'

I stood by the glass case, tapped on the side and said, 'He's called Harold.'

Alex looked round and raised his eyebrows. 'Harold? Harold the scorpion?'

For a moment I tensed.

Then he grinned. 'That's a cool name.'

I relaxed and took the hood off the tank so it was easier to see. 'It was Gareth's name for him.'

Alex was quiet for a moment, looking at the vivarium, but not moving.

'How is Gareth?' he asked.

For a moment I considered telling him about Gareth squeezing my hand, moving, but it didn't feel right. I didn't want to share that. Not yet.

'He's doing OK. He's still in hospital, but they say he's improving.'

Alex nodded and looked back at the vivarium. 'I really tried to get you out of there, you know. I just couldn't do it on my own. That's why I went for help. I didn't leg it.'

'I know.'

He paused. 'It was a good hideout though, wasn't it?'

I smiled and nodded. 'Yeah. Hell of a find.'

Alex came over to the vivarium and looked through the glass.

'Wow,' he said. 'Ugly little thing, isn't it?' He tapped the glass a couple of times then put his hand inside. As his fingers got close, the scorpion twitched and arched its tail ready for attack.

Alex laughed. 'Cool. Hey, Harold. How you doing? You gonna get me?' He wiggled his finger about in front of it.

I thought about Gareth, about the time I'd put my own hand in and picked the thing up. I could imagine him standing there, just like before, watching Alex doing the same, stupid thing.

I whispered, 'What do you think?'

Alex, thinking I was talking to him, said, 'He's cool.'

But I was talking to Gareth, because he was right there in the room. I didn't need to look up to know that. I could feel him, standing next to me, watching Alex and mulling things over. Eventually he said, 'I'm not sure.'

Alex turned, looked at me, 'What was that?'

'What was what?'

'I thought you said something.'

I felt my stomach tighten. 'I just meant he can be a bit boring. Harold. He's aggressive, but dull.'

Alex had his attention back on the scorpion. 'I think it's brilliant.'

But next to me, Gareth's voice, almost too quiet to hear, was full of concern.

'Be careful, Kyle. Be very, very careful.'

AUTHOR'S NOTE

Not many works of fiction are completely fictional. *Clash* is no exception. Many of the scenes were inspired by real events, most of which occurred years apart. The first was the mystery disappearance of my best friend.

We were both ten years old at the time, and had set out one day with the intention of getting utterly lost. We thought we'd managed it too, finding a wooded area on the far side of a place called West Park. We were clambering about, sliding down mud slopes and generally having fun when my friend, Wardy, simply disappeared.

I began to think he'd done a runner, when a voice from nearby said, 'I can see you!'

I looked around, but there was no sign of my friend. I could hear him laughing, and then his voice came again, 'Getting warmer.'

But no matter how warm I got, I still couldn't see him. Finally, a hand shot out of a load of ivy and pulled it apart, and there was Wardy hiding in a space under a rock, with a leafy curtain of ivy spilling right over the top. It wasn't exactly a cave, but he'd been completely hidden.

Twenty-seven years later, I started writing *Clash*. The hidden cave was the first scene I wrote, so I guess I owe Wardy some thanks for that brilliant vanishing act.

But I've got a few other people to thank too.

Ian and Ray Meston, for the amateur boxing nights. Occasionally, there was more fighting in the audience than there was in the ring. Parents screaming and shouting, drinks flying while two kids, both scared senseless, knocked seven bells out of each other.

Thanks to Tim Jennings for introducing me to cage fighting long before it became popular. I worked as an artist for Acclaim, and Tim was our IT technician, always ready to entertain us with tales of his fights, detailing styles and techniques and injuries.

A big thanks to literary agent Sarah Manson for believing in the story, taking me on, and doing all the complicated agency things people never hear about. And also to Non Pratt and everyone at Catnip for their enthusiasm, ideas and being so fantastic to work with.

I've got to mention Paula and our kids for putting up with me tapping away on this thing night after night, but especially Matthew, the driving force behind the words. What you lose out on in ability, you more than make up for in personality.

And what the hell – thanks to me too, for writing it!

Colin M, October, 2010

ABOUT THE AUTHOR

Colin lives in the North East of England with his wife and three sons.

When it became clear that his eldest son's cerebral palsy was profound, Colin left his job as an artist in the computer games industry to become a full-time carer. It was at this point that he began to take writing seriously, going back to basics and taking a professional approach to what had only ever been a hobby.

To keep the inspiration coming, Colin now works as a Teaching Assistant whilst his son attends school. Although he has a lot of fun at work, this leaves little free time for cooking, playing on the Xbox and juggling – but he always makes time for writing.

www.colinmulhern.com

To find out more about *Clash*, as well as
discover more exciting books, visit:

www.catnippublishing.co.uk